" When a book and a mind collide
with a hollow thud, the sound is
not always from the book. "

*- Lichtenberg*

# DEAR ME

## THE DIARY OF "DEAR JOHN" MACKAY

written & designed
by Michael Nugent

with Sam Smyth & Arthur Matthews

BLACKWATER PRESS

© 1994 Michael Nugent, with Sam Smyth and Arthur Matthews

Cover design Philip Ryan
Cover cartoon Aidan Dowling

Produced in Ireland by Blackwater Press,
Broomhill Business Park, Tallaght, Dublin

ISBN 0861216156

Dedication:

*To Anne and all at Willow Park*

Acknowledgements:

*To all who helped in any way in the production of this book, including Anne Holliday, Faela Smyth, Graham Linehan, John O'Connor, Anna O'Donovan, Hilda O'Sullivan, Philip Ryan, Eamon Cooney, Aidan Dowling and Tony Moreau.*

*And Joseph Nugent for minding the house when we were bringing the proofs to the publishers.*

**Michael Nugent** was born in Dublin in 1961. He is a graduate of the College of Marketing and Design, Dublin, and a co-founder of the New Consensus peace group. He has contributed articles and cartoons to various magazines and newspapers. He has completed a major study on the counter-screening of nuclear radiation through lead oxide. In 1986 he was a candidate for the position of Irish national soccer manager. In 1993, he co-wrote *Dear John - The John Mackay Letters* with Sam Smyth.

**Sam Smyth** was born in Belfast in 1945. He is an award-winning writer who has worked in New York and Dublin. In 1985 he wrote the script for a highly acclaimed RTE documentary on famine relief in Africa. He has written a biography of Charlie Bird, and both are convinced existentialists. Three years ago he was voted Ireland's "Journalist of the Year" for his investigative reporting of Irish business scandals. In 1993, he co-wrote *Dear John - The John Mackay Letters* with Michael Nugent.

**Arthur Matthews** was born in Drogheda in 1959. He is a graduate of the College of Marketing and Design, Dublin. He has been Art Director of *Hot Press* magazine, and has contributed articles and cartoons to *In Dublin* and *New Musical Express*. He has written several books on the assassination of President John F. Kennedy. He lives in London, where he writes television comedy scripts with Graham Linehan. In 1994, they co-wrote *Paris* and *Father Ted Crilly* for Channel Four.

# A MESSAGE FROM JOHN MACKAY

More than most people in Ireland, I empathise with Princess Diana and others whose private lives have been masticated by the molars of the media monster. Last Christmas my private letter collection found its way into the public domain when I foolishly allowed two apparently honourable gentlemen into my confidence at a select dinner party at my home.

As I recounted how I had spent 1993 writing to hundreds of prominent and influential figures and enclosing a fiver to grab their attention, I was momentarily distracted by a particularly unusual comment made by Senator David Norris, who was entertaining my dinner party guests with extracts from his one-man show "The Joyce of Sex".

I then discovered that I had somehow mislaid the mountain of missives which I had been showing to my two guests - who themselves also left in a hurry inversely proportional to that of an Irish soccer manager returning from Orlando for a welcome home celebration. Two weeks later my private correspondence was in the public domain under the title "Dear John".

I resolved this year to refrain from penning missives to people of note, confining my literary endeavours to keeping my personal diary abreast of events. Now that the year is over, it only remains for me to formalise the legal aspects of ensuring that this year's Mackay magnus opium remains confidential and private.

And my good wife Dympna has recommended for this purpose the reputable legal firm of Nugent Smyth and Matthews.

*John Mackay*

### Below:

The Great John Mackay DO-It-Yourself Euro-Funny-Money Animation Show:

### Instructions (option a):

Using thumb and forefinger, quickly flick through the pages of the book and watch the original £8 billion magically rise to £9 billion after devaluation of the punt, then equally magically fall to less than £6 billion as time goes on !

### Instructions (option b):

If you support Fianna Fáil or Labour, start at the other end of the book and watch the value magically rise instead of fall

**December 30: On This Day**

Feast of the Leaving Out of the Biscuits

Bank Holiday in Ireland, Mexico, Gibralter and parts of Portugal

**December 31: On This Day**

First Friday Of The Week

Mermaid discovered in Ballina reservoir, 1869

**January 1: On This Day**

Van Morrison enters moody period, 1965

Van Morrison celebrates twenty five years of moody period, 1990

ⓒ John Mackay

NEW YEAR RESOLUTIONS FOR 1994

December 31 1993

1. Keep up the poetry - buy a velvet smoking jacket and write at least one new poem a month.

2. GET FIT - do twenty minutes jogging every day in my new Shell suit.

3. Improve the neighbourhood as newly-elected chairman of the local Combined Residents Association Partnership (C.R.A.P.)

4. Get Dympna to design a nice C.R.A.P. badge for the breast pocket of my new C.R.A.P. regulation navy blazer.

5. Hand over the running of the Wolf-It-Down-Hound Bowl business to young Tobias in his new pinstripe.

6. Don't do anything as chairman of C.R.A.P. to assist Toby with the dog bowls (CONFLICT OF INTEREST!!!!!!!!!!!!)

7. Keep in touch with Uncle Pee over in Brussels.

8. Try not to fight too much on the C.R.A.P. committee with Dickie Mandate and his mates from the Red Rose Corporation Estate.

9. Have a good year (not bad nor indifferent) - Happy 1994!

> **80 per cent of air pollution comes not from chimneys and auto exhaust pipes, but from plants and trees**

*- Ronald Reagan*

John Mackay's "Things Not To Say" -

(No. 1 in a series)

Things Not To Say When Trying To Increase The Level Of Government Borrowing ...

"If you could just lend us another twenty billion, we'd be for ever in your debt "

### January 3: On This Day

Feast of the Good Angel of Electric Christmas Tree Lights

Length of Dublin Women's Mini Marathon increased to twelve feet, 1986

**Historians study released State papers from 1963**

### January 4: On This Day

Evening Press backs Castro with "We're Communists Too" front page headline, 1960

### January 5: On This Day

Moon in fourth quadrant after three in the afternoon

Twelve year old Patrick Pearse struck by acne, 1891

# NEW YEAR NEWSFLASH

1994 started today with the traditional release of State papers from thirty years ago. And 1963 was indeed a year of memorable events - in Britain, the Profumo scandal and the Great Train Robbery; in America, the Kennedy assassination and Martin Luther King's "I have a dream" speech .. and, in Ireland, the historically hysterical suggestion by a Senior Civil Servant that Saint Patrick's Day be relocated to September as March 17th was too associated with excessive drinking.

```
MEMO TO QUEEN MARY, PHOENIX PAR
FROM JOHN MACKAY

Re: moving St Patrick's Day; may I suggest
the following new calendar for September, a dull
month when life goes back to industrial sobriety:

Sep 1st      St Patrick's Day & World Cup matches
Sep 2nd      Christmas Day & All Ireland finals
Sep 3rd      Junior & Leaving Cert results
Sep 4th      January to August
Sep 5th      October to December
Rest of September      Hangover
```

## Wednesday 5

Snow closed the neighbourhood today, so I stayed in and reflected on how things can change in a year! It began with a simple one-page proposal to a Taoiseach who knew the difference between a Pal and a Chum. Now a new dogfood era has dawned - the Irish Wolf-it-Down-Hound Bowl is a howling success. And, to top it all, tomorrow I will finally be elected chairman of the Combined Residents Association Partnership. Life is good.

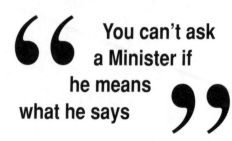

**You can't ask a Minister if he means what he says**

*- Seamus Brennan
at the Beef Tribunal*

*Thursday Jan 6:
I have to admit things were easier when we just had the Emerald Meadows Residents Association, but now of course we've been lumped in with the Red Rose Corporation Estate at the other end of town. So my Vice Chairman on the Combined Residents Association Partnership (C.R.A.P.) is Dickie Mandate from the Red Rose Estate.*

### January 6: Diary Entry

"Knock is great! I was walking out around the shrine today, and I thought, God, it'd be great crack to build an airport here, just for the laugh. Am I mad or what? Maybe some of the political parties would give me a few quid. A bit of clerical blackmail always puts the fear of God into them. Feck it! I'll write to them anyway."

*Monsignor James Horan,
January 6 1977*

### January 7: On This Day

Fifteen die as punk rock fever hits Castleisland, 1976

Lord Athlone forced to cut own lawn after angry walk-out by peasants, 1856

### January 8: On This Day

Quarter moon divisible by four in Gaeltacht areas

Leitrim abolished then reinstated after all-party negotiations, 1939

First Committee meeting of the year today. And
that Michael Wee the poet drives me crazy don't you know it. Still,
at least we've got Bertie Bucks as treasurer and An tAthair Smith
to keep relations with the church on an even keel. And young
Riffo Cowen will be on hand to do bouncer at the discos and to sort
out any aggro if the Red Rose lot get out of hand.

# CRAP

## the Combined Residents Association Partnership
### between Emerald Meadows and the Red Rose Corporation Estate

Minutes of First C.R.A.P. meeting of 1994

1. Election of Officers:
   Chairman: John Mackay, Emerald Meadows
   Vice Chair: Dickie Mandate, Red Rose Estate
   Treasurer: Bertie Bucks, Emerald Meadows
   P.R.O.s: Diggy Árlá and Spin Doctor Finlay

2. Election of Subcommittee Chairpersons:
   Neighbourhood Watch: Maire Go Go, Emerald Meadows
   Tidy Area: An tAthair Smith, Emerald Meadows
   Discos & Poetry: Michael Wee, Red Rose Estate
   Bouncer at Discos: Riffo Cowen, Emerald Meadows

3. The Chairman, Mr Mackay, told the Committee that,
   while he was Chair of C.R.A.P., he would take "no
   hand, act or part" in his family dogbowl business,
   which would henceforth be run by his son, Tobias.

4. The Vice Chairman, Mr Dickie Mandate, told the
   Committee that he could not hand over control of
   his used car sales business to any of his family,
   as they all had new secretarial jobs with C.R.A.P.

**Since a politician never believes what he says, he is surprised when others believe him**

*- Charles de Gaulle*

**January 10: On This Day**

Feast of Saint Dympna of the Perpetually Bewildered

Optional Bank Holiday in Spiddal

*John Mackay's Anthology Of Really Crap Jokes I Heard In The Pub This Year:*

*(No. 1 in a series)*

*A sandwich walks into a pub and says to the barman, "I'll have a pint, please", and the barman says "I'm sorry, we don't serve sandwiches"*

# Supreme Court to test Matrimonial Homes Bill

# Section 31 of Broadcasting Act to be dropped

**January 12: On This Day**

Gerry Ryan declares himself divine and without sin, 1987

Pearl Harbour attacked by some children with catapults, 1939

A SHORT POEM ABOUT A
MYTHICAL LEFT WING
RIGHTER OF WRONGS
ENIGMATICALLY CALLED
THE RED ROSE – THE
CHARACTER IS CLEARLY
FICTIONAL AND ANY
SIMILARITIES TO ANY
MOUSTACHIOED IRISH
TÁNAISTES, LIVING OR
DEAD LUCKY, ARE
PURELY COINCIDENTAL

THE RED ROSE

© John Mackay 1994

The Red Rose
Appears to many
To expose
Corruption any
Place he goes
With all his clan he
Takes good care of those
Ho ho

### ...y 11

The Supreme Court started
to examine the Matrimonial Homes Bill today. I
thought it was an alimony payment, but Dympna thinks that Queen
Mary may have wanted a clause inserted allowing all families, not
just her, to sack their servants. Also, Dympna went for a walk
today down by John Foregreenfield's house, and she swears that
the Foregreenfields have a mad uncle Gerry locked away in the
attic. I'll have to ask John for clarification on that.

### Wednesday 12

It seems the Foregreenfields do have a mad uncle
Gerry, who's working on a plan for world peace, and he's appearing
on the local community radio station, CRAP FM, later this week.
This has caused an awful fuss – not so much about him being able to
appear, but about who gets to interview him first. Dympna
suggested setting up a studio in a prison cell and letting Kevin O'Kelly
talk to him. Toby asked who Kevin O'Kelly was. Shut up, I explained.

" **Do you want an honest opinion or a politician's opinion?** "

*- Mary Coughlan TD*

Sat Jan 15:
Watched a great film today – "In the Name of the Truth". It's a true story about the need to distort the truth in a film to accurately tell a story about people distorting the truth in real life. I think. It's all very complicated anyway. But Dympna reckons it should be in line for several Oscars, including Best Film, Best Actor and Best Supporting Controversy.

8 billion

**January 13: On This Day**

Bob Geldof declared a Republic, 1977

Croke Park hosts Second Annual Festival of Begrudgery, 1946

## Tax Amnesty scheme a success, says government

**January 14: Diary Entry**

"Again, a day spent mostly counting. Counted up to twenty in the morning, continued to thirty in the afternoon, and was just about to move into the forties when Joan called me for supper. Some subtraction in the evening, followed by a short burst of multiplication before bed. I've to attend a ghastly meeting about Northern Ireland or something similar tomorrow, but I'll bring a piece of paper and a pen and do a bit of long division when nobody's looking."

*Garret FitzGerald*
*January 14 1985*

Good news today - the C.R.A.P. amnesty scheme has worked well, with furtive residents round at Bertie Bucks' house paying off fifteen percent of their overdue membership fees. Also, Dickie Mandate is back from Sith Ifrica, which is now a hive of Political Correctness (the P.C. lobby has been working like dermatologically-pigmentarily-enhanced-unique-yet-equal-individuals recently). Still it's not as bad as America. When Nelson Mandela visited there recently, a politically-over-correct reporter started a question with "Mr. Mandela, as an African-American, how do you feel about...."

As C.R.A.P. will be supporting the divorce referendum later this year, Dickie Mandate brought me along to a Red Rose Estate Workshop on Divorce. It was all quite good fun. We had to learn the following "Prayer For Divorce":

## RED ROSE ESTATE PRAYER FOR DIVORCE NUMBER ONE

Divorce is so good for young children
Though at first it may seem quite unpleasant
Because from now on every Christmas
They'll always get two sets of presents

### January 17: On This Day

Time of day "a matter for one's individual conscience" states Bishop, 1944

Restaurants serve food for first time, 1678

66 **The holocaust was an obscene period in the history of our nation ... in the history of this century ... We all lived in this century ...  I didn't live in this century** 99

*- J. Danforth Quayle*

John Mackay's "Things Not To Say" -

(No. 2 in a series)

Things Not To Say to a Judge from the Dock:

"Come outside and say that "

## Social Partners demand end to Probate Tax

## Post-Section 31 interview guide- lines announced

### January 20: On This Day

Children's sandals banned in Madagascar, 1964

**Monday 17**

Another C.R.A.P. Committee meeting today. Complaints about our plans for a Local Residents Probate Levy, which some of the residents are calling a "vampire tax" on the dead. Bertie Bucks defends the proposal on the basis that, if the dead can vote for us at elections, surely we can tax them. Dead right.

**Tuesday 18**

## OFFICIAL GUIDELINES FOR THE SAFE CONDUCT OF POST-SECTION 31 INTERVIEWS

1.  All interviews to be pre-recorded
2.  All interviews to be preceded by a nice cup of hot tea and fresh sandwiches
3.  No hard questions (e.g. what is the capital of Khazakstan, etc)
4.  Errmmm .... that's about it, really

**lay 19**

Every five years we get a chance to elect representatives to an international funding body for community groups. It is called the European Piggybank, and 1994 is one of its election years. Who will we run, I wonder? I hear that Dickie Mandate's lot will be putting forward Bernie Alone from the far edge of the Red Rose Estate. She seems a nice enough woman, not controversial at all. If she wins, she'll be on the pig's back.

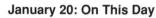

## " I'd like to be President .. you could take us anywhere, we'd know all the right cutlery and all that jazz "

*- Marian Finucane*

John Mackay's
"Things Not To Say" -

(No. 3 in a series)

Things Not To Say to Mary Robinson:

" Yes, love, I know you really wanted to go and chair that UN Committee, but you just have to realise that a woman's place is at home"

**January 20: On This Day**

Weather dull in places with temperatures likely to become higher inland

Hitler officially declared 'first citizen of Maynooth', 1944

**January 21: On This Day**

Full moon, big ring around Jupiter

Conor Cruise O'Brien completes difficult jigsaw with lots of sky in it, 1947

## Lorena Bobbit cleared in penis amputation trial

Our daughter Suzie moved back into the house today. It's her first year at College, and she had been staying in a flat with a friend – we had encouraged her to move out and earn her own living while she's still young enough to know everything. But apparently her flatmate kept borrowing her dresses and her makeup without telling her, and when Suzie complained about it, he would go into a sulk. So now she's back, and we had our first family dinner together since Christmas – myself, Dympna, Tobias and Suzie. And we reflected on how our lives have

**Friday 21**

changed in the past year, with the success of the Wolf-it-Down Hound Bowls. Naturally, none of us mentioned any loans Toby might be applying for for the business. As Dympna always says, that would be a passport to conflict-of-interest-land.

## STRANGE BUT TRUE STORIES BROUGHT TO MIND BY THE LORENA BOBBIT TRIAL

At a press conference after the death of General de Gaulle, his widow Madame de Gaulle was asked by a reporter what she wanted most during the rest of her life. In somewhat broken English, Madame de Gaulle replied " 'ap-piness " and was misunderstood.

" **Laws are like sausages. You sleep far better the less you know about how they are made** "

*- Otto Von Bismarck*

**John Mackay's "Things Not To Say"** -

(No. 4 in a series)

Things Not To Say to the West Midlands Serious Crime Squad:

Anything in an Irish accent

### January 24: Diary Entry

"Again, my brain became loose today during rehearsals for Tuesday's leadership speech. I've tried putting cotton wool in my ears to keep it in place, but that hinders my ability to hear the opinions of my front bench (not that I ever listen to them anyway). But if the old brain does come loose from its moorings and slip out on Tuesday I'll look rather foolish. So fingers crossed."

*General Eoin O'Duffy*
*January 24 1935*

## PDs tell Cox not to run for Euro Parliament seat

## Property Tax rise announced in Budget

### January 26: On This Day

Feast of short ankle socks

Half moon in places where full moon is not completely visible

**Monday 24**

Overheard a big row today while walking past the Progressive Detective Agency offices. They were telling Paddy Cox ha ha ha - their Member of the European Piggybank - that he couldn't run for re-election this time round. Why? Because he already had another job and anyway he said last year that he wouldn't run again for the European Piggybank. When I told the family about it over dinner, young Suzie suggested that they run their former chairman, Dessie Candoit, instead. Nonsense, I explained to the poor naïve girl, sure

**Tuesday 25**

Dessie also has another job - in fact, the same other job as Paddy Cox ha ha ha - and Dessie also said last year that he wouldn't run for the European Piggybank. And Dessie, whatever about Paddy, is an honourable man (I think it was Shakespeare wrote that about him). Poor Suzie, she understands so little of the real world.

Budget day! Sent a memo to Bertie.

```
MEMO TO BERTIE

FROM JOHN MACKAY          Dear Bertie,

RE: THE BUDGET           Very nice budget - especially
                      diverting the £5m property tax
                   into the redevelopment of The
                Croke Park Nursery For Potential
             County Councillors. Now a small
          request. We've had a family
       meeting and agreed to ban soccer
    and the RUC from our back garden.
   Is there any chance you might
  divert a few million our way?

     All the best, John
```

"" I have tried to smoke cannabis but since I cannot inhale I found it difficult to get any satisfaction from it ""

*- Ruairi Quinn*

John Mackay's Anthology Of Really Crap Jokes I Heard In The Pub This Year:

(No. 2 in a series)

"Knock, knock"

"Who's there?"

"O.J."

"O.J. who?"

"All right, you'll do for the jury"

**January 27: On This Day**

Dublin Bus "Exit by Centre Door Only" policy introduced, 1988

Mandatory death sentence for loose handshakes lifted in Arkansas, 1977

**January 28: On This Day**

Dublin Bus "Exit by Centre Door Only" policy abandoned, 1988

Bertie Ahern finds stain on tie, 1979

# Hume and Adams go to conference in America

**January 29: On This Day**

Decision taken to retain Dublin Bus "Exit by Centre Door Only" signs anyway, 1988

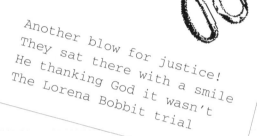

ODE TO THE TWO SUN JOURNALISTS
WHO (THIS IS TRUE) WERE AT THE
LIBEL TRIAL IN LONDON BROUGHT
BY EASTENDERS STAR GILLIAN
TAYLFORTH, AND WERE ASKED TO
DEMONSTRATE TO THE JURY WHETHER
IT IS PHYSICALLY POSSIBLE TO
PERFORM ORAL SEX IN A RANGE
ROVER

© John Mackay 1994

Another blow for justice!
They sat there with a smile
He thanking God it wasn't
The Lorena Bobbit trial

## y 28

Toby's in good form lately,
the Wolf-it-Down-Hound Bowls must be going
well, but naturally I don't know as I never speak to any
of the family about it. I now even refuse to read one-page memos
about the business, and I have nailed a large wooden partition
across the middle of the breakfast table. Met John Foregreenfield
this afternoon. He tells me he is off to America tomorrow to speak
at some conference or other on world peace.

### Sat/Sun 29/30

Dympna swears she saw a bearded man in a flash
Tíochfaidh Armani suit jump out of the Foregreenfields' attic window
and clamber into the boot of John's taxi to the airport. She rang
the Progressive Detective Agency, and they sent around the
fearless Gumshoe McDuel to investigate. He concluded that not just
the Foregreenfields' house, but the entire neighbourhood, would have
to be exorcised. I didn't realise we were all so unfit.

# Great Poetry Moments Of The Twentieth Century:

Michael Dee's Answer On Questions And Answers,
(Before Section 31 Was Dropped) When Asked If, As A
Government Minstrel, He Was Still Opposed To Section 31

*W*ell, first of all, you know,
responsibility for broadcasting
has not been transferred to me yet,
the order making that transfer
has not been made,
it will be made in the next few days,
that's the reality.

*A*nd the other point is, of course,
that the order precedes me,
and it's on the table of the Dáil,
and it would take a resolution of the Dáil and so on
to change that situation,
If one wanted to, because that's another issue...

*A*nd what I said in my statement,
which I issued only two days ago I think,
Was that I had little enthusiasm
for restrictions on broadcasting,
and I also had a respect for the
complexity of broadcasting issues,

*A*nd I'll be very direct with you,
    I said, I say in it,
       that the question of changing that policy
         would require very careful consideration,
       and he proposes to begin
         the process of consideration without delay,
       I'm certainly going to evaluate
         the operation of Section 31.

*A*nd what I have stated further than that,
one of my reasons are, is that,
  in relation to broadcasting,
     is a piece of broadcasting legislation
    the way to set about this,
      and I can, bluntly, my views haven't changed,

*T*hat I think it sits uncomfortably
  in broadcasting legislation,
    but I'm perfectly open, and I'm not,
     days before the order is made even
      transferring broadcasting to me,
going to prejudge anything,
  I am simply going to consider it,
   and I will consider it,
    and I'll look to it
      in its fullest and deepest sense,

*Y*es.

" **We had harsh words, I remember. He was saying I was petty and silly and schoolgirlish. I was telling him you're not so big yourself, you struck half the TDs off your Christmas Card list** "

*- Mary Harney on Charles J. Haughey*

**February 3: Diary Entry**

"The report has some unusual suggestions for cost cutting. One plan is for the top two steps to be eliminated from the stairways leading up to the aeroplanes. I vetoed this as it would require the passengers to leap a distance of over two yards into the aircraft, and the possibility of elderly or disabled individuals mistiming their jump and falling to their death would be greatly increased. There are, however, some other aspects of the report that could prove constructive."

*Aer Lingus official referring to report into greater efficiency, February 3 1973*

British Toady Minister Michael Portfolio claimed today that, when you do well in business outside England, it is because you are related to a Government Minister. Nonsense! Over here I'm sure you could get substantial investments for, say, a small dog-bowl factory, and it would be absolutely nothing to do with who your relations are.

**Business success linked to family connections**

Lots of news today. I read in the paper, at breakfast this morning, that public servants are to get an 11% pay rise after a six months pay pause. Fair enough, I commented. But will they do 11% more work? And will they confine themselves to a six months work pause? Also, Bill Clinton has dropped his ~~pants~~ plan for a Peace Envoy to give Northern Ireland back to the Republic. John Major has dropped his plan for a Peace Envoy to give Texas back to Mexico. And Mary Harmony has dropped her plan for a Progressive Detective Envoy to give Paddy Cox ha ha ha back to Fianna Fail.

MEMO TO JOHN MACKAY FROM DICKIE MANDATE

Re: CYCLING PLAN & ETHICS

Dear John,

I understand you intend to start cycling. No problem there. And I hear that when the local cycle shop offered you a free bicycle, you said it would be unethical to accept. Well done. However, I understand that, when the shop then offered to sell you the bicycle instead for £1, you said, grand, in that case, you'll take a dozen of them, then gave them £20 and asked for £8 change. Perhaps we could get together to discuss the subtleties of the forthcoming Ethics in the Residents Association idea?

Yours as ever, Dickie

66

## Power corrupts,
## but lack of
## power corrupts
## absolutely

99

*- Adlai Stevenson*

John Mackay's
"Things Not To Say" -
(No. 5 in a series)

Things Not To Say to
Patricia McKenna:

"But isn't chemical
testing on animals
good insofar as it
takes their minds
off how small their
cages are?"

---

**February 7: On This Day**

Michael McDowell hit by lightning for fifth time in three days, 1988

Fungi courted as possible Fine Gael candidate in Kerry local elections, 1973

## Opposition to budget Property Tax intensifies

## Seven Oscar nominations for top Irish film

**February 9: On This Day**

Bank Holiday in towns in Mayo that have a 'b' in their name

Twelve angry men calm down a bit, 1960

A SHORT POEM INSPIRED BY TODAY'S OPINION POLL ON REACTIONS TO THE BUDGET, WHICH SHOWS THAT THE PUBLIC ARE OUTRAGED BY THE SAVAGE IMPOSITION OF A PROPERTY TAX ON PEOPLE WITH HOUSES WITH MORE THAN THIRTY SEVEN BEDROOMS

ODE AGAINST THE PROPERTY TAX

© John Mackay 1994

Another budget where the sick
And poor get off scot free
They're lucky they've not got a big
Expensive house like me

Big international news today. Doctor Boutros Boutros Boutros of the Unexcited Notions warned the Bosnian Serbs to stop bombing Sarajevo immediately or else he'll get very very angry indeed and will hold his breath till he's blue in the face. The war ended at once, and everyone was happy. Rumours abounded that Dr Boutros Boutros Boutros may be nominated as the next Peter Sutherland. Also today, "In The Name Of The Truth" was nominated for seven Oscars, including Daniel Lay

Loose for Most Gratuitous Acts Of Masochism In Preparation For What Is Only A Film, After All, For God's Sake. Michael Wee has now convinced him to prepare for the title role in "In The Name Of the Party", by spending a decade talking through a certain part of his anatomy which would be better employed disposing of yet another of the tasteless chicken suppers he has to endure to build up support for his next party leadership bid.

> **The prospect
> of Fianna Fail
> examining the impact of
> the Maastricht Protocol
> on the Constitution is
> like a chimpanzee with
> a screwdriver
> at the back of
> a television set**

*- Michael McDowell*

John Mackay's
"Things Not To Say" -

(No. 6 in a series)

Things Not To Say to
A Government
Minister When She
introduces you to the
rest of the staff as
her new Secretary:

"Thanks, mum"

**February 10: Diary Entry**

British summer time begins, Irish summer time ends

Barry McGuigan prepares for World Championship boxing bout by hanging upside down from trees, 1988

Dana given freedom of Bucharest, 1970

## Fine Gael TDs rebel against Bruton leadership

## Labour nominates Guerin as possible Euro candidate

Michael Wee is actually doing a good job getting international films made over here. I cycled down today to see the filming of a new blockbuster - "The Blues Brothers". It is about two brothers, Johnny and Richard Blues, who are on a mission from God to save their political party from certain closure. But everybody is against them - and even some of their own party are trying to stop them succeeding. It seems like good fun.

A SHORT POEM INSPIRED BY THE ONGOING QUEST FOR CLARIFICATION ON THE THORNY ISSUE OF HOW THE PEOPLE OF IRELAND ALONE CAN EXERCISE THEIR RIGHT TO SELF-DETERMINATION

CLARIFICATION

© John Mackay 1994

Ireland was what the Irish made it
A place where only the Irish dwelt
Until the Irish were invaded
2000 years ago by the Celts -
(Celts Out - Peace In!)

Back to the real world. While I was down at the film set, Dickie Mandate and his friends at the Red Rose Corporation Estate quietly scored an O.G. by nominating her as a potential candidate for the European Piggybank elections. We responded immediately by selecting Olive Brazen as our electoral gender-mender (but only after Live-Line's Carry-on Finucane hung up the phone on us).

" You know, it's a pity about Ronnie - he doesn't understand economics at all "

*- Margaret Thatcher on Ronald Reagan*

**February 14: Diary Entry**

" 'Ah ... well, you never know ... yes, yes, yes ... ah, ha ... well, there's some that says it is and there's some that says it isn't ... yes, yes, yes ... well, you never know ... we'll see ...' This is the type of thing I can do in my sleep. In fact, I was asleep during the whole rehearsal."

*Cyril Cusack, on his first day on the set of Glenroe February 14 1986*

Wednesday 16th: Filming continued today at the Blues Brothers set, with Johnny and Richard Blues winning the first battle in their Mission from God - The Fantastic Four have retreated and the Titanic Two - Slaphead the DJ and Big Smokin Al - have sunk.

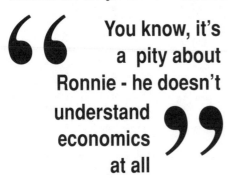

## Bruton beats Fine Gael rebels to win leadership battle

## Dukes concerned at "people talking about him"

**February 16: On This Day**

Cast of The Riordans mistaken for sharks while holidaying on Achill island, 1969

DID SOME RESEARCH IN THE LIBRARY TODAY ON GREAT
IRISH SURNAMES OF OUR TIME:

| | | |
|---|---|---|
| McEntaggart | Mac An tSagairt | Son of the Priest |
| McAnespy | Mac an Easpaig | Son of the Bishop |
| McForest | Mac an Fear Oráiste | Son of the Minister (Protestant) |
| Dingubber | Duine ag Obair | Son of the Minister (Government) |

There was a very dramatic
scene filmed today down at the Blues Brothers
film Set. Johnny Blues wanted to find out what his party members
thought about him, so he put on a disguise, then went down to a pub
and struck up some innocent conversation with a party member.
After a while, in a casual manner, he said "tell, me, what do you think
of Johnny Blues?" "Well, he's our leader" the man replied, "and we
always support our leader". "Yes, I know all that," said Johhny, "But
I've heard rumours of a minority dissident group who are trying to
subvert the majority wishes of the party". The man looked nervous
and whispered "it's not safe to talk here. Too many loyal people.
Come outside". So they went outside and the man said "it's still not
safe, come into this field". Then, in the field, the man said "it's still not
safe, come behind this hedge". Eventually, he lowered his voice still
further and whispered "You're right. I'm part of the subversive
minority. And here's the reasons why we support Johnny Blues ... "

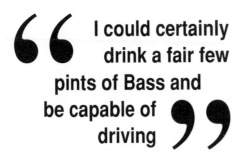

**" I could certainly drink a fair few pints of Bass and be capable of driving "**

*- Bertie Ahern*

<u>John Mackay's Anthology Of Really Crap Jokes I Heard In The Pub This Year:</u>

(No. 3 in a series)

A man walks into a pub with a newt on his shoulder called Tiny. The barman asks him "Why do you call it Tiny?" and the man says "because it's my newt"

**February 17: On This Day**

Little Big Horn officially twinned with Termonfeckin, County Louth, 1981

Green Shield Stamps "the horse cavalry of Satan's army" warns Pope, 1970

## Political dissident demands rights of travel and speech

## Mitchell agrees to stand as Fine Gael Euro candidate

**February 19: On This Day**

Toilet rolls replace leaves in Aras An Uachtarain washrooms, 1970

Eurovision song contest replaces map making as sixty seventh most popular leisure activity in Limerick, 1968

## AMNESTY SHOCK HORROR POLITICAL DISSIDENT IN INTERNAL EXILE NEWSFLASH

An international scandal has broken today about a political dissident in internal exile who wants to travel abroad to exercise her right to freedom of speech. However, the military junta in control of her small island insist that Queen Mary will stay in the domestic salt-mines of Phoenix Park, Ireland, where she has lit a symbolic candle in her front window to remind herself of those who were allowed to travel abroad.

**day 18**

Acres of agitation today
down at the Blues Brothers set, which they're
thinking of renaming as "Meath Streets". Big Smokin' Al started
complaining that people were talking about him. Then people
started talking about Big Smokin' Al complaining that people were
talking about him. Then Slaphead The DJ started complaining that
nobody was talking about him. And Mighty Mitch just started
complaining. Aren't thespians just so temperamental?

**Sat/Sun 19/20**

In a promotional stunt for the Blues Brothers movie,
the actor Mighty Mitch agreed today to stand as a Blues Brothers
charismandidate in the European Piggybank elections. He won the
nomination against an out-of-work writer called Vincent Browned-Off
after a competition to see who could name the most streets in
the constituency. Also today, Queen Mary started a public appeal
for a million pounds so she can buy an Irish passport and travel
abroad.

> **Republicans understand the importance of bondage between parent and child**

*J. Danforth Quayle*

**February 21: On This Day**

Bad moon rising

Pixies attack at dawn

Duck strike in St. Stephens Green enters fourth week, 1978

Tuesday Feb 22:
Black Tuesday. The High court was told today that the shares of Irish Depressed Newspapers are worthless. In scenes reminiscent of the Great Wall Street Crash, Despairing tycoons threw themselves fro the top floor of their Burgh Quay offices.

**February 22: On This Day**

Blue moon

Robot wins prize in Fleadh Ceoil, 1942

Wednesday Feb 23:
White Wednesday. The High court was told today that the shares of Irish Depressed Newspapers are worth £12 million. Dripping tycoons clambered out of the Liffey and struggled back to their Burgh Quay offices.

8 billion

# WHEN HARRY MET THE DISTRICT JUSTICE

Strange But True: In June 1973 five members of the Hare Krishna religion were brought to Dublin District Court to answer a charge relating to the adverse effect of their street celebrations on the sensitivities of some members of the passing public. With which of the following judicial sentiments did the wise District Justice send the tangerine-clad revellers on their way?

### Sentiment (a):

"As you may be aware, we in Ireland have a long history of fighting against religious persecution. Your religion, though it may be unfamiliar to members of the general populace, is as deserving of respect and freedom under the law as any other religion. I strike out the charges against you."

### Sentiment (b):

"Why are you dressed up in those ridiculous garments? I could sentence you for contempt for wearing a scarf like that ... I can warn you, you were lucky not to have been assaulted by the crowd. Any decent Irishman would object to this carry-on ... my only regret is that I can't have you locked up."

Answer: Yup, it's (b), I'm afraid (you didn't really have to check, did you?)

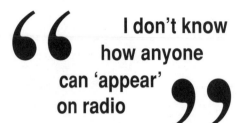

> **I don't know
> how anyone
> can 'appear'
> on radio**

*- Charles J. Haughey,
questioned in the Dail
on the appearance of
Fianna Fail Ministers
on pirate radio stations*

**February 24: Diary Entry**

"Another day chained to a radiator. I'm trying to teach one of the cockroaches Irish dancing. Around twelve I slagged McCarthy about being English. He hates that! Then I got him to test me on the capital cities of Europe. One of the guards is the image of Ken Barlow in Coronation Street. McCarthy doesn't think so, but he is. A bit of a treat in the evening as they allowed us to have bits of cardboard for supper."

*Brian Keenan,
February 24 1988*

*John Mackay's
"Things Not To Say"* -

*(No. 7 in a series)*

*Things Not To Say to
Gay Byrne:*

*"When man invests
money, God smiles"*

# Malone defeats Guerin at Labour Euro convention

# Surprise as Sinn Fein Ard Fheis seeks clarification

**February 26: Diary Entry**

"God, Brian Keenan is really annoying."

*John McCarthy,
February 26 1988*

### Thursday 24

Bernie Alone defeated the Red Rose brigade today to become their Dublin Euro-Piggybank candidate. Suzie suggested they run O.G. as well. Nonsense, I patiently explained. Dickie Mandate has made clear they will only run one candidate. And, as Shakespeare said, Dickie Mandate is an honourable man. As I reminded her, I've already explained all this political stuff when we were discussing the Progressive Detectives and Paddy Cox ha ha ha.

### Friday 25

## OFFICIAL: THE REALLY HARD QUESTION THAT WASN'T ASKED AT THE SINN FEIN ARD FHEIS

How come you can afford those flash suits and expensive haircuts and manicures when you're on the dole and when the price of clothes these days is daylight robbery?

### 26/27

Well, honestly. I'm scarlet with embarrassment. A prominent non-tabloid Irish newspaper of record today warned its readers that a Leinster House sex scandal is about to break. But surely that sort of thing doesn't happen in holy Ireland – The Leer Street newspapers boosting their sales by writing about sex, I mean.

> ❝ **A liberal is a man who is too broadminded to take his own side in an argument** ❞
>
> *- Robert Frost*

As usual, Michael Wee can always see the bright side. He's trying to talk Dickie Mandate and Jack The Law into co-starring in a new blockbuster Hollywood comedy movie about the European Structural Funds fiasco called "Honey, I've Shrunk The Quids".

**February 28: On This Day**

Half Day in Afghanistan on years ending in an even number

Leitrim Urban District Council elects first mountain goat, 1978

## Further confusion about value of structural funds

## Spring "resolutely opposed to privatisation"

**March 2: On This Day**

Tennis elbow responsible for over seven thousand man hours lost per year in Britain, states report, 1988

# CRAP

## the Combined Residents Association Partnership
### between Emerald Meadows and the Red Rose Corporation Estate

Minutes of C.R.A.P. Committee meeting, Feb 1994

1. Mr Bertie Bucks told the Committee that there is a massive amount of money missing from the grants C.R.A.P. was getting from the European Piggybank – in fact, the amount missing is so big that Bertie has run out of fingers to count it on. There was general agreement that the problem was very serious (not that the money was missing, but that we might have to admit it).

2. Mr Bucks suggested that we raise residents' membership fees to C.R.A.P. to make up the missing money. This suggestion was dropped when it was pointed out that the Committee members would also have to pay more. Mr Bucks apologised for the insensitivity of the suggestion.

3. Mr Riffo Cowen pointed out that C.R.A.P. gets half the takings from the public phone in the community centre, and suggested selling a percentage of the takings to somebody else. Mr Dickie Mandate loudly proclaimed that the Red Rose Estate members were "resolutely opposed to privatisation".

4. The Chairman, Mr John Mackay, suggested getting round this difficulty by calling it "a strategic alliance in the neighbourhood interest" instead of privatisation. Everyone laughed heartily and the meeting was adjourned until tomorrow.

**66** **And if they don't like it, then they can lump it** **99**

*- Pat Cox on his decision to redirect his ~~density~~ destiny*

John Mackay's "Things Not To Say" - (No. 8 in a series)

Things Not To Say to Ronald Reagan:

"Wake up, Ronnie, it's nearly four in the afternoon. And God says today is the day to push the red button"

**March 3: On This Day**

Summery weather denounced as "grievously sinful" by Free Presbyterian Church, 1890

Vagueness first used as device to avoid straight answer in political interview, 1767

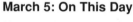

# Spring announces support for strategic alliance

# Top Irish Pol in Gay Park Probe Shock Scandal

**March 5: On This Day**

Nun topples into giant cake at Longford fundraising coffee morning for Fianna Fail, 1956

### Great Events On This Day
*Stranger Than Fact*

# CRAP

## the Combined Residents Association Partnership

### between Emerald Meadows and the Red Rose Corporation Estate

Minutes of C.R.A.P. Committee meeting, reconvened from yesterday

1.  The Vice Chairman, Mr Dickie Mandate, announced his full support for "a strategic alliance in the neighbourhood interest" between C.R.A.P. and any-one with a bit of money who wanted a share in the telephone takings. Everyone laughed heartily and the meeting was closed with everyone happy.

**y 4**

I told Dickie Mandate after today's meeting that I'd lost my bicycle, and he suggested I buy a car from his Honest Dickie's Used Car Sales Business. He said he's got a great car himself - the perfect car, in fact - painted red on one side and green on the other, so that the witnesses always contradict each other. Kind of like his politics, I joked. He didn't seem to laugh. Still, we seem to be getting on okay when you consider some of things he has said about me.

**Sat/Sun 5/6**

Another big news story this weekend! The Sunday Weird has a follow-up on last Saturday's Irish Times trailer with the first sizzling episode of the "Top Pol in Gay Park Probe" scandal. All sorts of comings and comings and goings are now going to be coming out. And, more importantly, I've remembered where I left my bicycle.

" **I don't give a shit about the Italian lira** "

*- Richard Nixon*

Wednesday March 9:
A bit of a shock today. Dickie Mandate added O.G. as a second Euro-Piggybank candidate. What next, I asked Dymphna over breakfast? Dessie Candoit replacing Paddy Cox ha ha ha? Young Suzie made the hilarious suggestion of Dessie Candoit running AGAINST Paddy Cox ha ha ha. Oh, how we all laughed.

**March 7: On This Day**

Greenhouse effect discovered in greenhouse in Ardfinnan, County Tipperary, 1987

Bicycle clips made compulsory for non-cyclists in Carlow, 1957

## Diplomatic Cox calls for outing of merciless bastard

## Labour add Guerin as second Euro candidate

**March 9: On This Day**

Ninth day of March

Mi-Wadi bottle spends record five hundred and second week in Kildare grocery store window, 1979

More Gay Park Probe Pol developments. Big Jim Commie from the Red Rose Estate called on the Gay Park Probe Pol to out himself. Then the Gay Park Probe Pol outed himself. Then the Progressive Detective Paddy Cox ha ha ha called on the merciless bastard who outed the Gay Park Probe Pol to out himself. Then a spokesperson for the Merciless Bastard Representative Body called on Paddy Cox to come outside and repeat that – and advised him to make sure his car is taxed and insured for the next generation

or so. Then Big Jim Commie clarified that, when he had called on the Gay Park Probe Pol to out himself, he was actually acting in the interests of the Gay Park Probe Pol, who had decided to out himself anyway, so his statement made no difference (then why did he bother making it, asked Dympna).
But it's no wonder so few gay people come out of the park if it's all so damn complicated.

THE PADDY COX HA HA
HA GUIDE TO EFFECTIVE
POLICE COMMUNITY
RELATIONS

No 1:

If you want to know the time, ask a merciless bastard

> **You're in RTE now, and it's 'eighteen *minutes*', and it's '*past* eight', not 'eighteen after eight'**

*- RTE producer reprimanding former pirate radio disc jockey Declan Meehan on the first day of Radio 2*

John Mackay's
"Things Not To Say" -

(No. 9 in a series)

Things Not To Say To Natalie Wood:

"What sort of wood doesn't float?"

**March 10: Diary Entry**

"A great day! I hammered a nail into my knee this morning and it was really sore! Then I went out for a long walk in sub-zero temperatures with no shoes or socks on. When I got home I cooked a great big plate of rashers, eggs and sausages and then threw the lot in the bin. Then I went to the pictures. When I got there, I wore a blindfold and stuffed pieces of rags in my ears so I couldn't see or hear anything. Fantastic! You never know, if I keep this up, they might name a bridge after me some time."

*Matt Talbot*
*March 10, 1912*

## Beef Tribunal costs to be higher than expected

## Labour announce Malone-Guerin "code of conduct"

I read in the paper today that costs may be higher than expected at the Bunburger Tribunal, which has been running far much longer than anyone expected when it was first set up. But my attention was distracted from the article by a big fuss and commotion outside the local shopping centre, where a small baby was choking while his mother screamed hysterically. Then a man dramatically rushed up and turned the child upside down, shaking him vigorously until he coughed up a small coin

he had swallowed. As the crowd cheered, the baby's grateful mother asked the man if he was a doctor. No, not at all, he replied, pocketing the coin, I'm a barrister from the Bunburger Tribunal.

## RED ROSE ESTATE
## CODE OF CONDUCT FOR
## BERNIE AND O.G.

1. Both candidates are equal, but one is more equal than the other

2. Voters will be asked to vote Labour 1 & 2 in order of our choice

3. That all seems fair enough, doesn't it?

4. If you don't agree, Bernie, you're off the ticket (erm... let's see if Pat Montague or someone can rephrase that one a bit before it goes out)

**"** **Diplomacy is the art of saying 'nice doggie' until you can find a rock** **"**

*- Will Rogers*

<u>John Mackay's</u>
<u>Anthology Of Really</u>
<u>Crap Jokes I Heard</u>
<u>In The Pub This Year</u>:

(No. 4 in a series)

A Moscow Communist called Rudolph looks out the window and tells his wife that it's raining. "No, Rudolph, it's snowing", she replies. He says "it's rain", she says "it's snow", and he says "Rudolph the Red knows rain, dear"

### March 14: On This Day

The moon's a balloon

The Derby allows horses to enter for the first time, 1868

Ancient Greeks discover the joys of fried tomatoes, 2000 bc

## Haughey attacks Labour "mercs & perks" culture

### March 15: On This Day

Three-cupped bras returned from shops in Dingle after design flaw discovered, 1990

### March 16: On This Day

Ham introduced into ham sandwiches, 1978

First horse to be trampled to death by jockey, 1943

Young Sean Haughty from across the road ~~made~~ didn't make a controversial speech today attacking Dickie Mandate's lust for power, mercs, percs, expensive hotels and scandals. He added that in these respects, the Red Rose Corporation Estate now leave our lot in the ha'penny place. I'll have to put young Haughty in his place - naturally, I am outraged at the implication that Dickie Mandate's lot leave us behind in any respect.

A SHORT POEM
INSPIRED BY THE
FACT THAT, EVER
SINCE THE LARK IN
THE PARK INCIDENT,
IRISH POLITICIANS
HAVE SHOWN A NEW
TOLERANT - AND
INDEED SUPPORTIVE -
ATTITUDE TO THE
QUESTION OF GAY
RIGHTS

ODE TO GAY RIGHTS
© John Mackay 1994

TDs are all
    for gay rights now
The reason why's
    a farce
They all think
    anal intercourse
Is talking
    through your arse

Strange But True facts: Young Sean Haughty was asked on the radio today whether the "ha'penny place" part of his non-speech was an admission that our lot were also associated with lust for power, mercs, percs and scandals. No, he explained, that part of the speech was to be taken with a grain of salt. But the rest of it? All true, he confirmed, with a perfectly straight face. Such style. A future Dickie Mandate.

**March 17: On This Day**

Cathal Brugha spends third day up oak tree in protest at treaty negotiations, 1921

Lone Ranger dons mask on permanent basis, 1890

"

# Hmmmmmm

"

*- Pat Kenny*

Sun March 20:
Bishop Jeremiah Hellfire this week prevented the local Mayor, Ian O'Protestant, from

## Reynolds visits America for Saint Patrick's Day

reading a lesson at the Mass which commences civic week. Of course, we all agree that Protestants should be allowed to take part in civic week masses, but only as part of an overall balanced constitutional settlement. I think that's what John says, anyway.

**March 20: On This Day**

Holy Day. No particular reason. It's just a bit holy.

A SHORT POEM INSPIRED BY A MEXICAN I MET IN AMERICA
WHO REFUSED MY INVITATION TO COME TO A BASEBALL
MATCH WITH ME

ODE TO JOSÉ THE MEXICAN

© John Mackay 1994

Said José, I'll not go
to the baseball with you
When I do, the crowd always mock me
First they stand up
so they all block my view
Then they all sing "José, can you see?"

St Patrick's Day in America!
Great fun, but when I got there, I was told the hotel
was full. Remembering the Waldorf Hysteria, I asked would they
have a room if Dickie Mandate wanted to stay the night. Their
demeanour changed immediately and they said "Dickie Mandate
from the Red Rose Estate? Of course, sir, that would be different".
So I said, fine, I'll take his room, he's not coming. Later, I was shown
all round the White House, from the Oval Office down to the hall
where Mister Clinton holds his balls and dances. I told them all
about the time I was behind in my taxes and I told the taxman
he'd get his money after I paid the banks. The taxman said he'd
get paid even if it was on my deathbed. So I replied, if I can
have it that long, you've got a deal! For some reason, President
Clinton didn't laugh, and neither did her husband – this Whitewater
business certainly has them in a black humour.

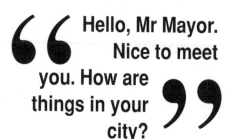

**Hello, Mr Mayor. Nice to meet you. How are things in your city?**

- Ronald Reagan, at a reception for black Mayors, to Samuel Pierce, his only black Cabinet Minister

**March 21: Diary Entry**

"I can't see a bloody thing any more. This morning I thought I was looking at a load of trees in a forest, but I found out later I was inspecting a guard of honour for President de Gaulle. I was talking to de Gaulle later on and was surprised to discover that he was French. He has very little Irish so we communicated by banging spoons over our heads."

*Eamon de Valera*
*March 21, 1970*

John Mackay's "Things Not To Say" -

(No. 10 in a series)

Things Not To Say To The Man Who designs The Benetton Ads:

"Here's a really mad idea - what about trying an ad with some Benetton products in it?"

**Paisley and Major discuss NI over tea and biscuits**

**Mitchell launches his Euro election campaign**

**March 23: On This Day**
Dawning of the Age of Aquarius

## TODAY'S STRANGE BUT TRUE COMPETITION

Ian Paisley today met John Major in Downing Street. One of them said afterwards: "I had to raise my voice in order that he could hear me because he was shouting so loudly" Was it: (a) Ian Paisley or (b) John Major?

(Answers on a postcard to the offices of the Deafened Unexpectedly Presbyterians, Coynie Ontrum, Norn Iron)

## TODAY'S STR... BUT TRUE COMPETITION

Bertie Bucks today said he was asking Davys Stockbrokers why they were reprimanded and fined by the London Stock Exchange. Was it: (a) Because they did something wrong or (b) because they told him to shove off and mind his own business?

(Answers on the back of a fiver to Bertie Bucks, C.R.A.P. Treasurer)

The Mighty Mitch today successfully launched the Blues Brothers Promotional European Piggybank Campaign by suggesting that the Attorney General was a communist philanderer who eats his own children. This followed Rule Number One of Attracting Obscenely Enormous Amounts of Unwarranted Publicity: to draw maximum attention to yourself, make an enormous mistake very publicly.

**March 24: On This Day**

Trees shed leaves in solidarity with Aer Lingus strikers, 1976

Furious Arabs attack Laois petrol station, 1973

*Sat March 27:*
*I went along today*
*with Dickie Mandate*
*to another of the*
*Red Rose Estate*
*Policy Workshops on*
*why we should*
*support the*
*Divorce*
*Referendum. Today*
*we all learned Prayer For*
*Divorce Number Two, which*
*tackles the legal implications of*
*this complex issue.*

## Mitchell in apology for Euro campaign launch

## Reynolds calls for resignation of Mitchell

**March 26: On This Day**

Hen wounded by duck in savage attack outside Dublin cinema, 1979

Bill to tax children at birth leads to Dail walkout by Labour Party, 1955

The Mighty Mitch today swung into action with Rule Number Two of Attracting Obscenely Enormous Amounts of Unwarranted Publicity: to maintain maximum attention on yourself after your enormous mistake, publicly apologise for what you say you now realise may be interpreted as the effect of what you said, but insist that you are essentially standing by the essence of what you say you said. Works every time - it's smokeless fuel for the "no smoke without fire" believers. Then I remembered

that the Mighty Mitch is chairman of the C.R.A.P. Finance Committee, so I quickly whipped off a letter to Johnny Blues demanding that he resign forthwith. Then I remembered Rule Number Three of Attracting Obscenely Enormous Amounts of Unwarranted Publicity: Provoke some naive idiot into calling for your resignation from something. Damn! Damn! Damn! Crap, total crap, even.

## RED ROSE ESTATE PRAYER FOR DIVORCE NUMBER TWO

Young children love custody battles
They think they're really cool
'Cause when they have to go to court
They get the day off school

> **I have opinions of my own - strong opinions - but I don't always agree with them**

*- George Bush*

Tuesday March 29:
I read in the news today that a new national agreement has been reached, whereby teachers who underperform or become surplus to requirements will now be entitled to retire early. Dympna pointed out that this scheme has been in place for some years in politics. It's called the General Elections and Ministerial Pensions Scheme.

**March 28: On This Day**

Feast of the Stuffed Olives

Sunday Independent does not publish article on alleged Van Morrison / Michelle Rocca bun fight in top Dublin restaurant, 1992

**March 29: On This Day**

Cow jumps over moon

Little dog laughs to see such fun

Dish runs away with spoon

**March 30: On This Day**

Sharp shift to the right, 1986

Average contents in baked beans cans 'on increase' warn Gardai, 1978

## Great Events
## On This Day
*Stranger Than Fact*

## Fitz Out
## Peace In

**O**ne of these leaflet designs is made up for fun, and would obviously never be used in real life. The other was used by supporters of a well-known Irish political party during the November 1982 General Election. Which is which?

THATCHER
WANTS
GARRET

DO YOU?

SAFEGUARD IRELAND'S NEUTRALITY

VOTE
Fianna
Fáil
The Republican Party

THE WAY FOR

WHO
LOVES
THE BRITS?
GARRET
FITZ

SAFEGUARD IRELAND'S NEUTRALITY

VOTE
Fianna
Fáil
The Republican Party

THE WAY FORWARD

Answer: the "Thatcher Wants Garret - Do You?" design was used in November 1982 on leaflets headed "Meath / Westmeath Fianna Fáil".

> " There are certain shades of the 1930's about them that I don't like, to be candid. Fascist tendencies. "

*- Brian Lenihan on the formation of the Progressive Democrats*

John Mackay's "Things Not To Say" -

(No. 11 in a series)

Things Not To Say To "An Post" Customers Angry at Postal Cutbacks:

"No, no, you'll still be getting two deliveries every day, it's just that from now on they'll both be delivered at the same time"

**March 31: On This Day**

Moon River

Mould on Roscommon man grows to size of small planet, 1954

Ships placed in water for first time, 1760

**April 1: Diary Entry**

"Woke up to be told that God didn't exist. Bit of a shock to the system. Apparently it was all over the early editions of the newspapers. Obviously thought of the inevitable effect on my career. Was just about to call a press conference when Cardinal Minetti came into the room. He tried to be serious at first, but couldn't keep a straight face. April fool! Silly old me completely suckered. Business as usual after that."

*Pope John Paul II*
*April 1 1980*

Former candidate publishes "Ten years hard Labour"

```
JOHN MACKAY'S BELIEVE IT OR NOT GREAT TRUE BUT
TOTALLY INNOCENT REAL-LIFE COINCIDENCES OF 1994:

Event: A raffle in the Law Library
Prize: A World Cup trip worth £4,000
1st prize: Albert Reynold's daughter
2nd prize: Justice Hamilton's brother
Tickets drawn by: Larry Goodman's Senior Counsel
(But sure isn't it a small oul' country after all?)
```

I told Dympna today that I'd had a
friendly lunch with Dickie Mandate, Johnny Blues, Mary Harmony and
Promises de Russia, and that we'd all agreed to put aside our
differences and work together for the good of the neighbourhood
until such time as the total C.R.A.P. bank overdraft was repaid.
Why, that's great, said Dympna, and so constructive and mature.
I'm so proud of you all. April Fool, I replied! Ho ho ho.

Bill Thorny, who recently moved out of the Red Rose
Estate, today launched a book titled "Ten Years Hard Labour"
(published by the excellent Blackwater Press, Dublin, Managing
Director John O'Connor, a very nice man indeed and only
coincidentally my own publisher). The book is an incisive insight into
why the Irish left isn't right and, though it doesn't say so, it reads
as if it could have been co-written by young Sean Haughty.

> **When we got into office, the thing that surprised me most was that things were as bad as we'd been saying they were**

*- John F Kennedy*

John Mackay's
Anthology Of Really
Crap Jokes I Heard
In The Pub This Year:

(No. 5 in a series)

A piece of string with a punk haircut goes into a pub where they don't serve pieces of string. The barman asks "are you a piece of string?" and the piece of string says "no, I'm a frayed knot."

**April 4: On This Day**

Two wheeled cars "could be a danger to road safety" claims A.A. safety expert, 1966

First slug found in lettuce, 1926

**Teachers want say in sex education guidelines**

**April 5: On This Day**

Feast of some Souls - the nicer looking ones

**April 6: On This Day**

First length of rope to reach ten feet, 1865

Pitchfork "a two pronged instrument with a wooden handle used mostly for agricultural purposes" declares Pope, 1789

Niamh Bhrassneck today proposed a new set of sex education guidelines to the local school committee. The teachers weren't overly impressed, and they responded with their own set of guidelines. Niamh eventually suggested that she would add their clause (4) onto her own to complete the guidelines. So everyone's happy now.

## THE OFFICIAL RED ROSE ESTATE "FACTS OF LIFE" EDUCATION GUIDELINES

1. You do .. you know, *that*
2. You have children
3. You get elected
4. You give them jobs

## THE EMERALD MEADOWS TEACHERS UNION "FACTS OF LIFE" GUIDELINES

1. You do .. you know, *that*
2. You have children
3. You get a job as a teacher
4. You spend loads of quality time with your children as you're on holiday for half the year

**We are so hell bent on assuming power that we are prepared to do anything for it**

*- Charlie McCreevy*

Sat April 9:
There was a big Turnup when the Eco-Warriors who live on the common had their Spring Solstice Think-In today. Following some optional opening incantations to the Gods of Muesli, they passed a series of controversial motions.

### April 7: Diary Entry

"Some of the lads were slagging me off this morning about the wart on my face. Bastards. Wait till I get them home! Everyone's in a really good mood and 'up' about everything. Nice afternoon tea in a charming little tavern type place near Kells. Excellent wholemeal biscuits. My favourites! The locals are very friendly. Looking forward to seeing Drogheda."

*Oliver Cromwell
April 7 1649*

# Surprise as Reynolds makes rare trip abroad

# Green Party conference urges new tax system

### April 9: On This Day

Moon obscured by Jupiter unless you've got really good eyesight or very strong binoculars

I went off to Cyprus today for a brief holiday with
Dympna and the thought struck me.. if we never came
back, who would miss us? We could be John and Dympna Valentine,
drinking wine by the sea while gazing at the sunset... then we could
open a squid-food factory, make a million, buy a passport and go
into politics. Sheer bliss. Or maybe we could pass on the idea to
Michael Wee for another film project.

## MOTIONS PASSED AT ECO-WARRIORS SPRING SOLSTICE THINK-IN

1. All cars to be replaced by sensible walking boots or sturdy tricycles with natural stabilizers
2. Equal rights for hedgehogs, parsnips, cabbage, ozone and other ethnic minorities
3. Protection of our neutrality with a very large hedge around the coast
4. Making fun of the eco-warriors to be made illegal, because IT ISN'T FUNNY (and because it's too easy)

/10

The Eco-Warriors
also caused some fuss when they
were reported as calling for additional taxation on
the C.R.A.P. Committee. But it later emerged that what they had
called for was an extra tax on fossil fuels, not fossilled fools.

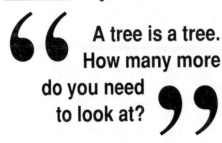

**A tree is a tree. How many more do you need to look at?**

*- Ronald Reagan*

Wed April 13:

There was a large release today of De Valera's old papers from the 1950's, when it seems he offered Ireland as a refuge to Pope Pius XII in the event of a Communist takeover of Italy. But the deal got mixed up, and instead Dev got a holiday in Italy, four gallons of holy water and a troupe of dancing statues in return for a constitutional amendment supporting a Vatican takeover of Ireland. Funny how history turns out.

# The Cheerio Haughty Computer Spell-checker

Cheerio Haughty's computer has a spell-check facility, which lists words similar in spelling to the words he types in. For which of our favourite politicians' names did Cheerio's spell-checker list the following alternative words?

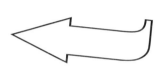

1. **Bartered Anorak**
2. **Seems Brimming**
3. **Join Broken**
4. **Glorious Colonies**
5. **Promises Russia**
6. **Virile Dolly**
7. **Ailing Duties**
8. **Patriot Flown**
9. **Cheerio Haughty**
10. **Muddledy Headings**
11. **Branded Healing**
12. **Gem Commie**
13. **Cheerily Microwaved**
14. **Mighty Nominee**
15. **Dizzy Homily**
16. **Merely Rerouted**
17. **Pithy Rebuttal**
18. **Blurt Remoulds**
19. **Merry Urbanising**
20. **Deck Sprain**

1. Bertie Ahern
2. Seamus Brennan
3. John Bruton
4. Gerry Collins
5. Prionsias de Rossa
6. Avril Doyle
7. Alan Dukes
8. Padraig Flynn
9. Charlie Haughey
10. Michael D Higgins
11. Brendan Howlin
12. Jim Kemmy
13. Charlie McCreevy
14. Michael Noonan
15. Dessie O'Malley
16. Mary O'Rourke
17. Pat Rabbitte
18. Albert Reynolds
19. Mary Robinson
20. Dick Spring

13

**❝ I was almost always certain that it wouldn't happen ❞**

*- Bishop Eamon Casey
on why he didn't
use condoms*

<u>John Mackay's
"Things Not To Say"</u> -

(No. 12 in a series)

Things Not To Say to
Robert Ballagh When He's Just
Finished One of His Paintings:

"It's all well and fine being able
to produce these super-realistic
paintings, but did you know you
can get the same effect these
days with a cheap polaroid
camera?"

**April 14: On This Day**

Charade of cornflakes being made from either corn or flakes exposed, 1987

Wildfowl announce their intention to boycott Montreal Olympics, 1976

## Sutherland gets GATT deal signed after 7 year delay

**April 15: Diary Entry**

"Caught Garrett adding things up again in his office. He pretended it was something to do with the Anglo-Irish agreement, but it wasn't. He had just taken a load of pencils out of a box and was counting them and was making notes on a piece of paper. I asked him to show me the piece of paper because I knew it was a load of multiplication or something, but he said it was top secret and wouldn't show it to me. I said that if it was top secret then I had a right to see it as I was Tanaiste, but then he mumbled something and tried to change the subject on to rugby because he knows I'm interested in that."

*Dick Spring
April 15 1985*

# CRAP

## the Combined Residents Association Partnership

between Emerald Meadows and the Red Rose Corporation Estate

Minutes of C.R.A.P. Committee meeting, Apr 1994

1. Several Committee members expressed concern that we are losing our sense of Irish identity through our dependency on the European Piggybank. Everyone agreed that we needed something that was part of our tradition and heritage to restore our sense of continuity with the past. Then news came through on the radio of a resolution to our problem - Irish Rail are preparing for a strike this weekend.

2. The Chairman, Mr John Mackay, told the Committee that Mr Squeaky Suds had completed some deal about a gate or a cat, or something that sounds like that anyway, and there is now more pressure on the Committee to nominate Mr Suds for President of the European Piggybank. The Vice-Chairman, Mr Dickie Mandate, told the Committee that he was working out some sort of a deal with a Mr Rude Rubbers from Holland, who also wants this job. Mr Mandate will have details of the deal available next week.

3. Neighbourhood Watch: Mrs Maire Go Go told the Committee that Teagasc is seeking a licence to grow cannabis at its research centre in Carlow, to investigate its potential in making teabags. The Committee agreed to ask the Gardai drug squad to have a word with Mr Barry in Cork about this matter.

" **Pat's gonna win. I'm gonna see to it. I don't care where I have to break in** "

*- G. Gordon Liddy, of Watergate burglary fame, endorsing Pat Buchanan for President of America*

John Mackay's "Things Not To Say" -

(No. 13 in a series)

Things Not To Say to Prionsias de Rossa:

"Any chance of an autograph? I know you're busy, so can you just put it here on the bottom of this letter and I'll leave you alone"

8 billion

**April 18: On This Day**

Blinking rapidly in public de-criminalised in Cuba, 1980

Jerry Lee Lewis lost in carpark for third week, 1957

## Under strength Irish team shocks Dutch in 1-0 win

**April 20: On This Day**

Twink narrowly avoids collision with nuclear missile after airport mix-up, 1987

Dickie Rock "fifth most well-known person in the world", claims survey, 1973

MEMO TO DR HOWLING FROM DICKIE MANDATE

Re: WORLD CUP RAFFLE PRIZE

Dear Brendan,

I understand you have won a raffle prize of a package holiday for two to the World Cup in America. Well done! I also hear that you intend to give the prize back, as you cannot go. I see what you are trying to do, but have you have read our proposal for Ethics in the Residents Association? If you cannot go, you must surely have a family member you could give the prize to. If not, you might consider giving it to one of the other families from the Red Rose Estate. Remember, ethics starts at home!

Yours as ever, Dickie

I asked Dickie
Mandate today about the deal
he said he had made with the Dutch last week in return
for our supporting Rude Rubbers as President of the European
Piggybank. He assured me it was all sorted out, and that the
payment would come through tomorrow.

Olé, Olé Olé Olé, Dickie's deal with the Dutch came through today.
Holland 0, Ireland 1 in Rotterdam - and with half of our first team
injured! I asked Dickie if the deal carried through to let us win if we
played Holland in the World Cup as well. Safe as the eight billion, he
replied. So we all went to bed happy tonight.

> **You have to keep young hands and young minds busy, and if you don't, some of them will go the other way**

*- Padraig Flynn*

John Mackay's "Things Not To Say" -

(No. 14 in a series)

Things Not To Say to John Gormley:

"That Adolf Hitler was a vegetarian too, you know"

**April 21: On This Day**

Moon visible if looking upwards

Longford dog sues owner successfully over unsatisfactory kennel conditions in landmark legal case, 1968

## "Airplane" star Leslie Neilson visits Dublin

## Gormley to be first Green Lord Mayor of Dublin

**April 24: On This Day**

St. Derry of Derrynane's birthday, 789 (if he was still alive)

Moore Street was packed today for a visit from Leslie Neilsen, the star of the Airplane and Naked Gun films. His co-star wasn't here, but that didn't matter, since nobody has ever heard of him – some bloke called O.J. Simpson. ("something serious has just turned up, O.J., you'll have to go to court" "Court? What is it?" "It's a big red brick building with a judge and a jury and loads of television cameras, but that's not important now")

A SHORT POEM INSPIRED BY THE SILVER-TONGUED ELOQUENCE OF THE AVERAGE PROFESSIONAL FOOTBALLER WHEN BEING INTERVIEWED AFTER A GAME

THE FOOTBALLER'S POEM

© John Mackay 1994

Well basically Brian
Wacko's done well to cut inside
The gaffer's over the moon
I've timed me run to perfection
And then I've gone off to me
grammar class

The Eco-Warriors today selected John Reasonable Gormley to be the first ever Eco-Mayor of the neighbourhood. He said he was not a fanatic, that he would alternate use as appropriate between the Mayor's car and his Victorian tricycle, and that while he personally was a vegetarian he would respect the right of guests to have meat on the menu or cull baby seals in the front hall if the etiquette of the occasion demanded.

**66** **Let's try winning
and see what it
feels like. If we don't
like it, we can
go back to our
traditions** **99**

*- US Democratic Party
Presidential candidate
Paul Tsongas*

John Mackay's
"Things Not To Say" -

(No. 15 in a series)

Things Not To say To
The Management at
Irish Steel:

"Well that's the way
we've always done it,
and frankly I can
see no good reason
to change now"

**April 25: Diary Entry**

"Apparently I've been managing the
Republic of Ireland rather than
Northern Ireland. I remarked to an
official that Belfast seems very quiet
despite the troubles and he told me
we were in Dublin. We're playing
someone tomorrow that starts with 'D'
(Denmark? Doncaster Rovers?
Probably one of those, can't think of
anything else), so I'll have to bloomin'
interrupt my fishing to fit that in."

*Jack Charlton
April 25 1987*

# Flynn concerned
# at Sutherland
# speculation

# First democratic
# South African
# general election

**April 27: On This Day**

Ronald Reagan slurs three thousandth
word as President, 1981

2 billion

A SHORT POEM IN SESAME
STREET STYLE INSPIRED
BY TWO TIMELESSLY
INSPIRATIONAL VIRTUES,
EVIDENT IN EVERY EPOCH
OF THE HISTORY OF
HUMANKIND; THE VIRTUES
OF SELFLESS HONOUR AND
PERSONAL SACRIFICE IN
THE INTEREST OF THE
GREATER GOOD OF THE
WIDER SOCIETY

ODE TO UNCLE PEE
© John Mackay 1994

Uncle Pee
Appointee
Oversea
Full of glee

Sudsie plea
Pedigree
Pee: Gimme!
Guarantee

Today is the dawn of our freedom'
said Nelson Mandela on the day of Sith Ifrica's first
multi-racial elections. It has been a truly joyous month. All races
and tribes have been represented. At times, some members of the
minority Sith Ifrican White, Coloured and Black tribes could even be
spotted here and there, but they faded into numerical insignificance
beside the majority Irish Broadcasters and Political Observers tribe.
Sadly missing were some of our election observers, who were
caught wearing ANC tee-shirts and dancing the toyi-toyi at ANC
rallies. Idiots. Don't they know the First Golden Rule Of Anything At
All To Do With The Fair Conduct Of Elections - DON'T GET CAUGHT.
Contenders for the John Mackay Sith Ifrican Election Top Tans
competition: John Bowman, Pat Cox, Martin Cullen, Austin Currie,
Brendan Daly, Tony Gregory, Helen Keogh, Derek McDowell, Nora
Owen, Rory O'Hanlon, Shane Ross and many others. And the winner:
Charlie Bird, just beating Moosajee Bhamjee into second place.

66 **I'm not particularly critical of Fine Gael except insofar as Alan Dukes and Garret FitzGerald are Fine Gael** 99

*- Gay Byrne*

<u>John Mackay's Anthology Of Really Crap Jokes I Heard In The Pub This Year:</u>

(No. 6 in a series)

What does a Dublin Northsider say in a traffic jam?

"Press or Herald !"

**Shergar owners fail in court compensation bid**

**Ireland complete hat-trick of Eurovision wins**

**April 30: On This Day**

Optional Bank Holiday - if you feel like it. No pressure.

2 billion

The shareholders in Shergar today failed in a damages claim for an insurance payout they never got when the horse was stolen. The court had problems reconciling the conflicting evidence of two expert witnesses: the West Midlands Serious Crime Squad, who said that the Birmingham Six had stolen the horse, and the Gardai Heavy Gang, who said that Alderman Nicky Kelly had kidnapped it and hid it in a fifth floor flat in Ballymun.

## VATICAN NEWSFLASH

The Pope, who slipped in his bathroom last night, had an operation today on a fractured thigh. He had to be taken away from writing his new encyclical, "Why People Who Use Condoms Are Committing Mortallers By Artificially Dabbling With Nature". Doctors report that he won't be able to get back to writing it until he gets used to his new artificial hip.

30/1

The Government has won the Eurovision Song Contest for the third time, outperforming the previous Government's victories in the Tour de France and the Italy World Cup. Cherie Riyon assisted with a mastery of French pronunciation that awarded two of our rivals twelve bridges and eight peas respectively - somewhat like John F Kennedy when he told Berliners, in flawless German pronunciation, that he was a hamburger.

" An independent
is the guy who
wants to take the
politics out
of politics "

*- Adlai Stevenson*

John Mackay's
"Things Not To Say" -

(No. 16 in a series)

Things Not To Say On
a Job Application To
The Green Party:

"Hobbies and
Interests - culling
baby seals"

**May 2: On This Day**

Overly sweet chocolate disgusts
Wicklow man, 1890

Coats first used as makeshift
goalposts, 1876

ICTU celebrate
centenary with
May Day parade

Roddy Doyle in
"Family" drama
controversy

**May 4: On This Day**

St. Augusta's Day

Take care on the roads

A SHORT POEM, TEMPERED BY AN UNJUSTIFIED
CYNICISM ABOUT THE SELFLESS CLASS STRUGGLE OF
THE TRADE UNION MOVEMENT, AND INSPIRED BY TODAY'S
HUGE MAY DAY PARADE, WHICH CELEBRATED THE
CENTENARY OF THE IRISH CONGRESS OF TRADE UNIONS

M'AIDEZ

©John Mackay 1994

Comrades we must celebrate
In true trade union way
One hundred years of struggle -
We'll do fuck all work today

**y 3**

Roddy Doyle week started
today. The nation was shocked by a television drama which
shattered the image of one of Ireland's most sacred institutions.
The language and behaviour was so gratuitously offensive that even
Gob Geldof phoned in to complain. But RTE refused to bow to
fundamentalist pressure, and vowed to continue to broadcast
highlights of the Garda Representative Association conference.

**Wednesday 4**

Half of the attendance at the G.R.A. conference
walked out of the hall today when rumours spread that Paddy Cox
ha ha ha was outside. And a district justice said that people who
didn't believe that scenes like those happen in real life should come
into court any day and listen to the proceedings. Roddy Doyle is
busy working on the script for the sequel: "Son Of Paddy Cox ha ha
ha's Merciless Bastard - G.R.A. Conference, The Reconvening".

> **He went to great pains to assure me that I hadn't been struck off the list and that everyone else had got one. And I said no they hadn't, and started naming off the people who hadn't either**

- Mary Harney on
Charles J. Haughey's
Christmas Card list

Friday May 8:
Some Election Trouble for
Pat Run Rabbitte Run. The
Progressive Detectives
are complaining that he's
using their corporate colours
of blue and yellow instead of
the traditional communist red
hammer and sickle

**May 5: Diary Entry**

"I'd never seen a real car before, but dere were loads of dem outside Heuston Station. I tought dat dey would look like de ones in De Flintstones and de driver would have to run really fast to move it, but it had a ting called an 'injun' which makes it move. Den it was on to de RTE studios! Wow! Dere really big! Den it was in to see 'Gaybo' and De Late Late Show. He is brilliant! We saw ourselves on de TV monitors and waved a lot at dem so dat people at home could see us. Den we went home."

*Un-named former
Fianna Fail Minister for
Communications,
Date unknown*

## Labour Party hold "mid-term think-in"

**May 6: On This Day**

Leeds 1 Arsenal 0

Solicitors and lawyers become universally unpopular, 1860

There was, of course, another heated family drama this week – Dickie Mandate brought the Red Rose Estate brigade for a day-long "mid-term think-in" in Killiney. I have studied their list of priorities, and I have no problems at all with them:

### RED ROSE ESTATE MID-TERM "THINK-IN" DELIBERATIONS

1. Don't rock the boat
2. Keep Uncle Pee out of harm's way over in Brussels
3. Do whatever is needed to keep Uncle Pee over in Brussels
4. Yes, of course, that means that Squeaky Suds can't have that job
5. Keep talking about other things to distract attention from priorities 1 - 4
6. What other things?
7. Errmmm ... privatisation, third banking forces, that sort of nonsense
8. That's that sorted out, then. Anyone for champagne?

> **You might be interested to know that the scriptures are on our side on this**

*- Ronald Reagan
on the United States
arms build-up*

Wednesday May 11:
More Election Trouble
for Pat Run Rabbitte
Run. Suzie's mob in the
local students union
Gay and Lesbian
Society are
campaigning against
his offensive and
intolerant poster
slogan "Straight Talking"

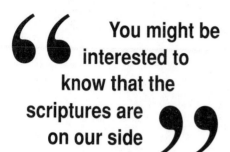

**May 9: On This Day**

Moon moves in with Jupiter and her husband, Frank

Pigs give one eyed farmer the runaround in inaugural Waterford farmer/pig hide and seek competition, 1980

*Speculation on Sutherland job bid intensifies*

**Thousands attend Kevin Moran testimonial game**

**May 11: On This Day**

God help us all

Went down to the film set today to see how they're getting on with the Blues Brothers. They were filming a scene in which one of the rebels, Alan Shatstir, was complaining that adoption laws give the parish priest more power than the natural father. He was supported by the campaigning pressure group "Hierarchy For Hierarchy In The Hierarchy," who pointed out that such a rule could have caused serious seniority problems in the Justin Casey case.

A SHORT POEM INSPIRED BY INTERNATIONAL FEEDBACK I HAVE BEEN RECEIVING (WHICH COMPLETELY CONFIRMS THE UNSUITABILITY OF SQUEAKY SUDS AS A REPLACEMENT FOR JACK THE LAW)

WHAT THE FOREIGNERS THINK OF SUDS

ⓒ John Mackay 1994

They think in every foreign city
Suds should be in the loony bin
They always look at him with pity
And say "look at the State he's in"

Went to Lansdowne Road today for Kevin Moran's testimonial game. I hate the way ordinary football fans have to put up with the attention-seeking antics of a small unrepresentative minority, who have no interest in football, but who just latch on the occasion to draw attention to themselves. Well, they were all here again today - every one of the Euro-Piggybank candidates, handing out their campaign leaflets outside the ground.

**"** We have no room in this country for Nazis and we are not going to entertain them here **"**

*- Oliver J. Flanagan on the purchase of Irish land by German citizens*

John Mackay's "Things Not To Say" -

(No. 17 in a series)

Things Not To Say To Bishop Eamon Casey on his first day in Ireland after being allowed to return home:

"Congratulations! What are you going to do to celebrate?"

2 billion

### May 13: Diary Entry

"Friday the thirteenth. Unlucky for some. Including me. Spent the entire day locked in a cupboard. Food was fed in to me via a long piece of plastic tubing. No solids - just soup, powdered meats, etc. An address to the Catholic Boy Scouts was carried out despite the fact I was locked in the cupboard. I was simply loaded onto a lorry and driven to Athlone and I talked to them through the keyhole. Celibacy, hell, 'watch out for women' etc. The usual stuff. Then home to a supper of liquid carrots and sherry."

*Archbishop Charles McQuaid May 13 1955*

## Cox quits PDs to be independent Euro candidate

## "Renewal Ard Fheis" for Fine Gael in Limerick

### May 14: On This Day

Paul McGrath goes missing for entire season, 1986

It's four weeks today to the European Piggybank Elections, so I had a go at the banks for making large profits. That always goes down well. And Ruari Rua suggested that C.R.A.P. should set up a special fund to give cheap loans to small businesses in the area. Must remember NOT to tell Toby in case he applies for a loan for the dog-bowls. I'll tell him this afternoon that I'm not going to tell him about it. That should do the trick.

Another huge row down at the Progressive Detective Agency today. Dympna was walking by when she heard them rehearsing a pantomime - you know, "Oh yes I will" "Oh no you won't" "Oh yes I will", that sort of thing - then Paddy Cox ha ha ha stormed out the door with a suitcase and jumped on the bus to Cork. Dympna thinks she heard him muttering something about fulfilling his density.

## BLUES BROTHERS NEWSCLASH

Fine Gael's dramatic "Renewal Ard Fheis" today had everything: anticipation, thrills, crowds and sustained cheering, all of which testified to the perfect timing skills of Johnny Blues and his team. Unfortunately, it was all directed at the telly, where Man United were playing Chelsea in the FA Cup Final in a tragic clash of events which, to be fair, could only have been foreseen by somebody living in the real world (by the way, the blue shirts lost at Wembley, too)

"" I hope I stand
for anti-bigotry,
anti-Semitism,
anti-racism ,,

*- George Bush*

*John Mackay's*
*"Things Not To Say" -*

*(No. 18 in a series)*

*Things Not to Say To*
*a Caller to The*
*Samaritans:*

*"Yeah, yeah, yeah,*
*sounds really bad, but*
*frankly, you know, it's*
*not my problem"*

**May 16: Diary Entry**

"It's a mad world, all right. Mad, mad,
mad, mad, mad, mad, mad, mad. With
loads of mad people in it. Mad, mad,
mad, mad, mad, mad, mad, mad. Sure
we're all a bit mad, really."

*Dr. Anthony Clare*
*May 16 1999*

## Spring calls on Sutherland to clarify intentions

## Spring clarifies his own intentions about Sutherland

**May 18: On This Day**

Entire population of Roscrea admitted
to regional mental hospital, 1960

Decline in standard of table manners
noted in Claremorris, 1958

This Squeaky Suds business is getting out of hand. Dickie Mandate is under pressure to support him as the new boss of the European Piggybank, and Uncle Dee is starting to panic and preach at me. Anyway, since Squeaky is too ~~cowardly~~ coy to announce that he wants the job, Dickie decided to call his bluff by asking him to declare himself interested or else get off the pot.

## PROGRESSIVE DETECTIVE DEFECTION NEWSFLASH

Shock waves still reverberate throughout town following the decision of Paddy Cox ha ha ha to privatise himself in his quest for a European Piggybank seat. "This is scandalous behaviour - refusing to support the party leader or accept democratic party decisions, then walking out to do his own thing" complained Mary Harney. "It goes against everything Des O'Malley and I had in mind when we started the party."

Nice one Dickie. After Squeaky Suds called his bluff by declaring his interest in the top Euro Piggybank job, today was both the best and the worst day of Dickie Mandate's life. The best, because he managed to ensure that Uncle Dee would be kept out of the country for the foreseeable future. The worst, because, in order to do that, he had to publicly declare that he was happy with Uncle Dee's performance. Ho ho.

**"** In my day if a guard told you to fuck off, you fucked off as quick as you could **"**

*- Charles J. Haughey*

<u>John Mackay's</u>
<u>"Things Not To Say"</u> -
(No. 19 in a series)

Things Not To Say To
Jackie Charlton:

"Good news! We've hired a geneologist to investigate your Irish ancestry, and it seems you're related to a family called the Dunphys"

2 billion

---

**May 19: On This Day**

Extra butter on sandwiches

Sexy man walks down Grafton Street to cries of "he's a bit of all right" from local girls, 1978

## Ahern welcomes reported upturn in Irish economy

**May 21: On This Day**

Crow from Wanderly Wagon enters Saint John Of Gods for alcohol treatment, 1972

---

**May 21: On This Day**

98 per cent of prisoners in Mountjoy prison "sing themselves to sleep", states report, 1942

Wednesdays introduced into annual calendar, 1813

Young Suzie has come up with a new colour-based theory of political divisions in the neighbourhood. Ourselves Alone and the Eco-Warriors are both using green posters; The Blues Brothers, the Progressive Detectives and Pat Run Rabbitte Run are all using blue and yellow posters; and the Red Rose Estate lot are using red (or is that just blood?). She reckons her theory is much more accurate than anything she's seen before, and she's doing her college thesis on it.

I had some good news for today's C.R.A.P. meeting - business is going great throughout the neighbourhood.
That's bad news, explained Bertie Bucks. The better we do, the less money we get from the European Piggybank. And then Dickie Mandate will leave us all in the lurch. So now we have to ensure that business goes badly. I'll get young Riffo Cowen to have a word with the lads down at Dreamer Lingus.

## THE PADDY COX HA HA HA GUIDE TO ALL-TIME FAVOURITE CLASSIC FILM GENRES

1: Science Fiction
2. Cowboys and Indians
3. Merciless Bastards and Robbers

# Well, if I had, I wouldn't tell you

*- Bill Clinton, asked by a reporter if he had ever had an extramarital affair*

John Mackay's Anthology Of Really Crap Jokes I Heard In The Pub This Year:

(No. 7 in a series)

A baby owl says "what! what!" and his mother says "no, it's hoo! hoo!" and the baby owl says "what! what!" and his mother says "haven't I always told you, it's 'hoo', you know, not 'what', you know"

**May 23: On This Day**

Full moon followed by half moon

Half moon followed by little girl on pony

## Publication of "Ethics in Govt" bill expected soon

**May 23: Diary Entry**

"Everywhere there is devastation. Bare foot children came up to me on several occasions and begged me for money and food. In parts of the town, blood is literally flowing in the streets. I saw several locals with knives sticking out of their necks and stomachs. Most of the natives seem to communicate without a recognisable language, using grunts and groans instead of words. Accommodation is reasonably cheap, though."

*Tim Bleeker, reporting from Limerick for the BBC's Holiday Show, 1988*

The Committee had a first look today at a report on the Ethics in the Residents Association Bill, which the Red Rose Estate lot seem to insist is needed. Most of it seems okay, but we may have to change some of it.
I don't know.

## RED ROSE ESTATE "ETHICS IN THE RESIDENTS ASSOCIATION" PROPOSALS

1.    Committee members must declare all of their interests in the neighbourhood, and all of the interests of their spouses

2.    Committee members may not tap the telephones of other residents or secretly tape private conversations with each other

3.    Committee members, or their friends or election agents, may not vote twice at C.R.A.P. elections, or telephone residents at 3 in the morning of the day of the election, loudly seeking support for another candidate

4.    Committee members may not, under absolutely any circumstances at all, be caught doing any of the above or it will be even worse as we will have to create the impression of doing something about it

**May 26: On This Day**
Birds start to fly, 1784
First ceremony takes place, 1609

> **At the time both were made, both were correct**

*- Seamus Brennan explaining contradictory statements to the Beef Tribunal*

John Mackay's "Things Not To Say" -

(No. 20 in a series)

Things Not To Say To Gary Kelly:

"I don't care if you <u>have</u> scored against the world champions, it's way past your bedtime and you're coming off that pitch and going home IMMEDIATELY "

Reynolds in "Irish passports for investment" row

Soccer shocker as Ireland beats Germany 2-0

**May 28: On This Day**
Tides available after lunch, maybe

A SHORT POEM INSPIRED BY THE GRANTING OF THE FREEMANSHIP OF DUBLIN TO THE SECOND IN OUR LONG LINE OF NATIONAL SAINTS BORN IN BRITAIN

DUNPHY'S DREAM

© John Mackay 1994

Though none dare call him negative
About our players' skill
When asked to name
his World Cup team
Big Jack replied "Brazil"

**y 27**

I knew it! I knew they'd do something like this! The Progressive Detectives have had gumshoe McDuel poking about for weeks, down by the holiday home that the Miseries have bought, and now in his typically bizarre way he's trying to link it with some loan the Miseries gave to young Toby down at the Wolf-It-Down Hound Bowls factory. But I know nothing about the loan! If there is one, that is, I mean, of course.

**Sat/Sun 28/29**

Another great soccer win today – 2-0 against Germany. We are now clearly favourites to win the World Cup – indeed, anyone who says otherwise is either a treasonous traitor or the national team manager. While I was in a soccer mood I started to read the diaries of the former Leeds United striker Alan Clarke, but it turned out to be about a different Alan Clark who was much more prolific at scoring and was rarely known to keep a clean sheet.

**" Politics is perhaps the only profession for which no preparation is thought necessary "**

*- Robert Louis Stevenson*

Tuesday May 31:
Only a week and a bit to go to the European Piggybank Elections. We're doing okay, apart from John Stifford, who seems to be everywhere but whose campaign has been a bit two-dimensional, and of course Olive Brazen, who's doing crap, total crap - but then there's women for you.

### May 30: On This Day

Moon falls out of sky

Supernatural meaning interpreted by three Spanish schoolchildren

**"Irish passports for investment" row intensifies**

### June 1: Diary Entry

"I was thinking today how brilliant I am. I decided to ask some of the cabinet how brilliant they thought I was. Everyone said they thought I was brilliant, and that was exactly what I wanted to hear. Gerry Collins seemed to hesitate for a moment, but he'll probably change his tune when we come nearer to the next cabinet reshuffle. Michael Woods seems to think I'm completely brilliant altogether. He must be looking for the finance job. Anyway, the general mood seems to be that I am absolutely fucking brilliant altogether. Which, of course, I am."

*Charles J. Haughey*
*June 1 1980*

## Great Events
## On This Day
*Stranger Than Fact*

**Monday 30**

This Miseries affair just won't go away. Those bloody Progressive Detectives! Everything that goes wrong these days is their fault, and they've been even more intolerable since Paddy Cox ha ha ha privatised himself. Still, I suppose you can't blame them for being upset – I mean, that sort of thing hasn't happened to any party in the neighbourhood since... erm.. well, errmmmm.... that's right, since Michael Keating did exactly the same thing to them a couple of years ago. ho ho.

**Tuesday 31**

## HELP WANTED - BRIGHT BOY OR GIRL FOR DEPUTY LEADER

TEMPORARY POST (SEASONAL) - TRADITIONALLY LASTS UNTIL THE DAY NOMINATIONS CLOSE FOR THE NEXT ELECTION

Apply to: Mary Harmony or Gumshoe McDuel at the Progressive Detective Agency

**y 1**

An tAthair Smith explained today that, when he met Mr Miserie, he thought he said he was living alone, not giving a loan, so he didn't like to pry further, as he might have had to explain our divorce laws. And Dickie Mandate had a look at the files and he's completely happy with that explanation. (I often wonder is there nothing that Dickie won't profess himself happy with? Still, who's complaining? certainly not Dickie anyway).

" **In most cases it is self-induced through gambling or drinking** "

*- Brendan McGahon on poverty*

**June 2: On This Day**

Ku Klux Klan registered as official charity in Ennis, 1946

Greed replaces shoplifting in official "Seven Deadly Sins" list , 1789

Sunday June 5th:
The soccer team today surprisingly lost against the Czech Republic, which seemed to actually

**Ireland bounced by Czechs in final pre-USA match**

please Big Jack, though then again he did think ( yes, this is true) that we had lost to someone called Yugoslavia. Of course, that could have been because the Garda band ( yes, this is also true) played the Slovakian national anthem instead of the Czech one before the game. At least they didn't play the British anthem for us (though I suppose the players might have known the words to it if they had).

2 billion

# SEX APPEAL

4/5

$N$ow that we've got your attention, perhaps you might consider voting for Orla Guerin in the European Elections on June 9th?

(And that Malone woman as well, if you really feel you have to)

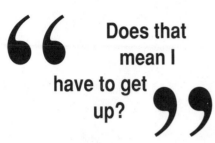

## Does that mean I have to get up?

*- Ronald Reagan on being reminded on waking up that it was his inauguration*

Today's Red Hot tip:
Bet on Bernie Alone
to beat O.G. in the
European Piggybank
Election - Dickie
Mandate keeps
trying to get the
two of them
together for a joint
photocall, so I think
we can assume Bernie is well
ahead there.

**June 6: On This Day**

Athlone celebrates liberation from indians, 1834

Running away first used as means of getting out of trouble, 1767

## Stafford in Euro Election leaflet controversy

## Stafford in second Euro Election leaflet controversy

**June 8: On This Day**

First completed javelin throwing event on moon, 1974

New three sided shamrock introduced in Galway, 1914

Got a leaflet today from John Stifford, with a cartoon of Big Jack voting for him - which is likely to be counterproductive, as Big Jack never gets anybody's name right (Suzie reckons Stifford would do better using a cartoon of Eamon Dunphy voting for all of the other candidates). Then Big Jack attacked Bernie Alone for issuing the leaflet and she started to cry and got lots of sympathy from everybody.

7

**❝ ASK NOT WHAT YOUR COUNTRY CAN DO FOR YOU, BUT WHAT YOU CAN DO FOR JOHN STIFFORD ❞**

"On June 9th, like Jack Charlton, I'll be undertaking to vote number 1 for John Stifford - As I always say, Ich bin ein Fianna Fáiler. God Bless Ireland"

*John F Kennedy*

ay 8

Got another John Stifford leaflet today, this time with a cartoon of Dana voting for him. I rang him up to remind him that it was the Rock 'n' Roll kids who won this year's Eurovision, but he said he was trying to remind people of the days when we used to have an overall majority. I suggested that, if he wanted to go back that far in time, he should use a cartoon of Brian Boru voting for him.

**You know
what I want.
What do
you want?**

*Charles J. Haughey's
opening line to Tony
Gregory in 1982*

**June 9: On This Day**

President de Valera blames wife
Sinead for continuous drafts around
house, 1920

Air replaces earth in balloons for first
time, 1914

Sat June 11:
Got an angry phone call from
Uncle Pee over in Brussels,
complaining that his
daughter wasn't
elected. I asked him
would he like to come
back and show us how
it should be done, but
he suddenly went
quiet and hung up the
phone.

## Shock as Greens' McKenna tops Euro-poll

## Malone beats Guerin for final seat in Dublin

European Piggybank Election Day! And you always
meet lots of interesting people on Election Days! On the
way down to vote, I met one of Charlie Haughty's old friends, I think
he used to be involved in some of his election campaigns. Nice man.
Then in the afternoon, I met him again, and he was wearing a false
nose, moustache and glasses. And on the way home, I bumped into
him again, and he was dressed as a woman this time. Funny man.
Afterwards I went along with Dickie Mandate to one of his Seminars
on Why We Should Support Divorce.

**Friday 10**

RED ROSE ESTATE
PRAYER FOR DIVORCE
NUMBER THREE

D ivorce is so good for young children
Though their family was sacred before
They've now got two mommies and daddies
So they've doubled their sacredness score

11/12

The European
Piggybank Count was bizarre!
Bernie Alone has beaten O.G. and one of the Eco-Warriors - a painter
called Patricia Mckelangelo - has TOPPED THE POLL. I asked had young
Mckelangelo painted the glossy soft-focus Mona Lisa reproduction on
the wall, but I was told that was an election poster for O.G. Still,
Michael Wee seems delighted at the result. He's making notes for a
future film project - Thelma and Louise Hit Brussels.

**"** A victory of
good over
evil, of freedom
over tyranny,
of peace over
war **"**

*- J. Danforth Quayle on the
Gulf War*

*John Mackay's
Anthology Of Really
Crap Jokes I Heard
In The Pub This Year:*

*(No. 8 in a series)*

*When golf first started, one
under par was a birdie, two
under was an eagle and three
under was a partridge. Then
they had to change the rules,
because you couldn't get a
partridge on a par three*

**June 13: On This Day**

Feast of Sandwiches

Galway Urban District Council appoint
first lion tamer west of the Shannon,
1962

### Jobs crisis hits
### Team Aer Lingus
### and Irish Steel

**June 14: Diary Entry**

"Still arguing privately that a Hydrogen
bomb is essential for Ireland's
defence. Who knows Wales' long term
plans? The Isle Of Man, though small,
can also look extremely threatening.
And of course, perfidious Albion, the
old enemy, lurking in the background,
always a threat. Essential that we are
not caught 'on the hop' and have to
defend ourselves with pikes and a few
Mausers left over from the Howth
landings of 1914."

*Sean MacBride
June 14 1950*

A NEW VERSION OF THAT BLOODY "ROBIN HOOD"
SONG THAT MIGHTY MITCH HAS BEEN BLARING AT
US THROUGHOUT THE EURO ELECTION CAMPAIGN

© John Mackay 1994

Mighty Mitch, Mighty Mitch, Riding through the glen,
Mighty Mitch, Mighty Mitch, Chased by the A.G.'s men,
Worse than being caught he
Lost to Bannotti
Mighty Mitch, Off the pitch, What a ...(shame
it'll look like a cop-out if this
line doesn't end with bitch)

# CRAP

## the Combined Residents Association Partnership

### between Emerald Meadows and the Red Rose Corporation Estate

Minutes of Emergency C.R.A.P. meeting, June 14

1. Bertie Bucks stressed the urgency of closing
   down some businesses soon, or else we'll be
   doing too well to qualify for our European
   Piggybank money. Immediate priorities:

2. Riffo Cowen is to close down Dreamer Lingus,
   while Ruari Rua gets ICTU to intervene. One
   option: replace the management with some of
   the airport kitchen staff who have spent
   millions paying £20 for £7 boxes of tomatoes.

3. We probably won't have to do much with Irish
   Steal, as they're doing a good enough job of
   closing that down themselves.

4. Next C.R.A.P. Committee Meeting - Saturday
   afternoon, outside Giants Stadium, New York,
   as that's where most of us will be (of course,
   we may have to travel earlier to acclimatise)

**"** **They have no sense of humour at all. We certainly have the best jokes** **"**

*- Tomas Mac Giolla
on the Progressive
Democrats*

*John Mackay's
"Things Not To Say" -
(No. 21 in a series)*

*Things Not To Say To
Patricia McKenna:*

*"Sod the rain forests.
Why not save some
place sensible where
the weather is
decent and civilisation
has emerged ?"*

**June 16: On This Day**

Generous mouse donates Lotto winnings to charity, 1990

The phrase "this so-called 'enlightened' age" used for the first time, 1947

## Barworkers to strike on day of Italy match

## Ireland beat Italy 1-0 in opening World Cup game

**June 18: On This Day**

Raisins banned as contraceptive devices in Italy, 1914

Excellent news today - Dreamer Lingus may be on strike from Monday, there's a SIPTU strike out in Coolock, Irish Steal are selling off some of their land, the barworkers strike looks like going ahead, AND - an added bonus - B+I ferries are also going on strike! Some days everything just goes just right. A few more weeks like this and our European Piggybank money will be as safe as the proverbial eight billion.

## BEYOND "OLÉ, OLÉ" - THE SPOOFER'S GUIDE TO SEEMING TO UNDERSTAND THE COMPLEXITIES OF THE WORD CUP

1. The Germans always do enough in each round to be there or thereabouts
2. The Africans and the Asians are great to watch, but so naive in defence
3. The colourful Brazilians are the team all of the neutrals want to see win it
4. England are shite

Olé, Olé Olé Olé.

Ireland 1, Italy 0. Naturally, I had to attend, since our last chairman, Charlie Haughty, was so prominent when we beat Italy 0-1 during the last World Cup. The Italians held no surprises for Big Jack - as he said, he can see them on Sunday morning telly most days of the week - but I was surprised at how hot the stadium was, as I was sure Bertie had told me that the heat was in tents.

> **There are two periods when Congress does no business: one is before the holidays, and the other after**

*- George Prentice*

**June 20: Diary Entry**

"Chance of a 'leg-over' situation with Kitty O'Shea on Tuesday, so I'll try and skip the Parliamentary Party meeting. What are we discussing on Tuesday anyway? Painting the postboxes green instead of red. Not exactly worth getting shot over. No, I'll call round to Kitty, and have a bit of a chat, then maybe we'll go out for a drink in Kitty O'Shea's (now there's a co-incidence, eh?)"

*Charles Stewart Parnell*
*June 20 1888*

John Mackay's
"Things Not To Say" -

(No. 22 in a series)

Things Not To Say To Ben Dunne when he tells you the weather is great in Orlando:

"I bet you sort of miss the snow, don't you?"

# Charlton wins World Cup water row with FIFA

# Job losses begin at Team Aer Lingus, Irish Steel

**June 22: On This Day**

Feast of Maltesers

6 billion

**Monday 20**

Ole, obey obey obey! FIFA today told Big Jack he couldn't throw water bottles to the Irish players. And back home, several hundred Dreamer Lingus staff are to be laid off. Some of the Red Rose Estate reps on C.R.A.P. are objecting on the grounds that, once Dreamer Lingus starts laying off workers, more job losses will inevitably follow – their own. I suppose that's what's meant by workers' solidarity.

**Tuesday 21**

Obey? No way no way no way! Big Jack seems to have won the Battle Of The Water Pressure with FIFA. He can throw plastic waterbags to the players. But throwing of bottles is banned, said a FIFA official later on this afternoon from his hospital bed. Big Jack was later spotted smiling as he ticked off a name in a little black notebook – obviously picking the team for Friday.

22

A SHORT POEM, PENNED AS DREAMER LINGUS HAVE STARTED LAYING OFF WORKERS, AND AS RUARI RUA HAS MADE CLEAR THAT IRISH STEAL MAY CLOSE COMPLETELY, SEEKING TO CAPTURE IN POETIC FORM THE SOMBRE MOOD OF A SHATTERED NEIGHBOURHOOD

IRELAND, JUNE 1994

© John Mackay 1994

Dreamer Lingus jobs are gone
Irish Steal's in tatters
But since the World Cup is still on
IT DOESN'T FUCKING MATTER!!!!!!!!!

**❝** **We want to dehumanise the social welfare system** **❞**

*- Albert Reynolds*

John Mackay's "Things Not To Say" -
(No. 23 in a series)

Things Not To Say To An Irish Steel Craftworker:

"Isn't it terrible the way people without unions are forced to do a week's work before they get paid?"

**June 23: On This Day**

Wichita linesman becomes full referee, 1974

Head lice "rampant in Gardai" claims report, 1966

## Ireland lose to Mexico despite late Aldridge goal

## Norway game now crucial for qualification

**June 26: On This Day**

Cemeteries closed for annual redecoration in Munster

Ballroom dancing outlawed in Burma, 1960

MEMO TO JOHN MACKAY

FROM THE FAI,
ORLANDO

Dear John,

Glad you enjoyed the Italy game
- things have certainly changed
since the days when two dozen
people would pack Dalymount for
Ireland against West Germany
Reserves! Now soccer is the
ultimate Irish family game -
and, to prove it, we've given
two match tickets (and a photo
opportunity) to Bishop Justin
Casey!

No way, dismay
dismay dismay! Despite the water win,
we were washed out today by the Mexican waves and a canary-
clad goalie who gave us the bird. And Big Jack had to be restrained
from having a quiet word with a FIFA official who was rehearsing a
Roddy Doyle script with Alamo Aldridge - who then scored a goal
that brought mixed feelings. The bad news is we'll have to stop telling
that joke about the Birmingham Six, on their release from prison,
asking "has John Aldridge scored for Ireland yet?" The good news is
that the goal could get us through to the next round - young Toby,
who has a pocket calculator and a part-time degree in algebra, has
worked out that we can still qualify if we draw with Norway next
week by a score that is evenly divisible by the square root of the
hypotenuse of the half-time score of Italy's game with Mexico on
the same day, if Venus is on the cusp of a raspberry jam sandwich
and a cup of tea (which is actually less complicated than some of
the permutations we used to have to worry about in pre-ole days).

**June 27: On This Day**

Moon sold to Johnson and O'Brien in bakery buyout, 1962

Athlone recaptured by Indians, 1960

" **Tell me, General, how dead is the Dead Sea?** "

*- George Bush to Jordanian Chief of Staff*

John Mackay's
"Things Not To Say" -

(No. 24 in a series)

Things Not To Say To Albert Reynolds:

"Hey, dad, you're not going to believe this, but I just got a phone call from some foreign bloke who wants to give us a loan of half a million quid!"

**EU meeting fails to agree on Delors replacement**

**Ireland qualify for second round of World Cup**

**June 29: On This Day**

President Robinson enveloped in shaving foam during official visit to factory, 1993

6 billion

Yesterday's meeting in Corfu failed to find a replacement for Jack The Law. The result was nine nations supporting Unlucky Dehaene, two nations supporting Rude Rubbers, and one nation each (the United Kingdom and the Irish Times respectively) supporting Leon the Brit and Squeaky Suds (does this put Suds in the Two Nations league?) So now everyone is hassling me again about Suds and his stupid damn gate deal.

## BEYOND "OLĒ, OLĒ" - 5 OF IRELAND'S GREATEST EVER SOCCER VICTORIES

1. 1993, in Windsor Park: 1-1 against Northern Ireland
2. 1990, in Italy: 1-1 against England
3. 1990, in Italy: 1-1 against Holland
4. 1990, in Italy: 0-1 against Italy

   (a "moral victory"- a footballing term for a victory in which your opponents score more goals than you do)

5. 1988, in Germany: 1-1 against USSR

Ole, halfway halfway halfway! Today we had our most recent greatest ever victory in world soccer history. With Jack In The Box confined to the stands, a modern-day monk in the round tower overseeing the latest battle against the vikings, we emerged triumphant to dramatically win 0-0. Apart from the absence of any goals, it was a victory to compare with any of the great wins listed above! It's a funny old game.

**"** **Is it the case that every time somebody calls for a vote they lock the door in case somebody else comes in?** **"**

*- Alan Shatter on voting procedures for the Dail Joint Committee on Legislation*

John Mackay's
"Things Not To Say" -

(No. 25 in a series)

Things Not To Say To Boris Yeltsin:

"We're well past the time now, Mr Yeltsin. Have you not got an airplane to go to ?"

6 billion

**June 30: On This Day**

Sand on Irish beaches "made up of tiny rock particles" claims UCD study group, 1969

Sean Doherty overcomes temptation to tell first fib, 1952

# Labour "Team" rebel TDs defy government

# Surprise as Dail adjourns for long summer break

# the Combined Residents Association Partnership

### between Emerald Meadows and the Red Rose Corporation Estate

Minutes of C.R.A.P. Committee meeting, June 1994

1. The Vice-Chairman, Mr Dickie Mandate, arrived late, and explained that he was just back from New York, where he had been watching the Ireland Norway game. Mr Riffo Cowen asked Mr Mandate had he not said before the Italy match that he would stay at home if the residents wanted him to. Mr Mandate replied that he had promised to stand for change, and he had now changed his stand on that promise, but he was being consistent since they were still the same words, just in a different order.

2. The Chairman, Mr John Mackay, referred to the recent vote in which four of the Red Rose Estate representatives sought to keep Dreamer Lingus open. He reminded the Committee that our high level of European Piggybank funding depends on us remaining economically incompetent. The Vice-Chairperson, Mr Mandate, gave a commitment to publicly discipline the members concerned.

3. Meetings were adjourned until mid October, to allow Committee members to fly off to the sun on full pay and expenses. Some members pointed out that the Progressive Detectives have complained about these long holidays. The Chairman, Mr Mackay, replied that nobody else would notice as THE WORLD CUP IS STILL ON AND NOTHING ELSE MATTERS!!!!!!!!!!

> **The Russians cannot vastly increase their military productivity because they've already got their people on a starvation diet of sawdust**
>
> *- Ronald Reagan*

**July 4: On This Day**

Feast of money

Holy Day in America

Sharks repelled by smelly Kinsale fishermen, 1890

John Mackay's Anthology Of Jokes That Are So Brilliantly Crap That They Just Had To be Included Even Though They Wouldn't Fit On One Page

(No. 1 in a very short series)

**Confusion over world cup welcome home celebration**

Two professional golfers are talking in the clubhouse. One says to the other "I had the most amazing thing happen to me today. A chap challenged me to a round of golf for £500, but because I was a professional he wanted two 'gotchas' as a handicap" ....

(continued on next left hand page ...)

6 billion

We're finally out of the World Cup, beaten 2-0 by reality, despite a late disallowed goal when one of Paul McGrath's knees broke away from him when it caught sight of the bar. Poor Packie was so shattered after the game that he tried to end it all by jumping in front of a bus, but luckily the bus went through his legs. I was so shattered I ended up using the above joke, which is infinitely worse than the result of the game. As is now usual, the streets of the neighbourhood were totally deserted during the game, apart from the young Eco-Warrior Patricia McKelangelo who was pacing up and down the empty footpaths - having topped the poll in the Euro-elections after refusing to watch the count, she was trying to work the same voodoo for the team by not watching the game. I'm always intrigued by these primitive Eco-superstitions. Then she was off to City Hall, where her fellow Eco-Warrior John Reasonable Gormley became our first Eco-Mayor (and the most succesful by far of the boys in green this week).

MEMO TO JOHN MACKAY
FROM BIG JACK, ORLANDO

Dear John,

Got your invite to the big party on Thursday. Sorry I can't come, but I'm contracted with Guinness or the Sunday Independent to do some fishing - or is it to commentate on a football match? I don't know. Anyway, hope everyone back home in Iceland has a great time. See you soon.

All the best, Big Jack

**"** **Nowadays the fundamentalists have gone up-market with a lead from the Knights** **"**

*- Michael D. Higgins*

*(... continued from previous left hand page)*

.... The golfer continues "Now, I presumed a 'gotcha' was something like a 'gimme', so I said fair enough. Then, on the first tee, just as I'm in the middle of my swing, he reaches between my legs from behind, grabs me hard, and shouts gotcha!" And the second golfer says "That must have been painful. I assume it made you even more determined to beat him" ....

*( continued on next left hand page ...)*

**July 7: On This Day**

First woman appears drunk in public, Ballycastle, County Antrim, 1690

Cabbages become available in leaf form, 1473

**Charlton returns for Welcome Home celebration**

**July 10: On This Day**

Height seen as advantage over width in Attractive Girls Competition, 1890

I went down to the Park today for the Welcome Home celebration. There must have been at least seven million people there, if there were five thousand. Gary Kelly and Jason Macateer were specifically introduced as the two teenybopper hearththrobs of the team, but for some inexplicable reason they insisted on bringing some coloured lad called Babb up with them. Do they not know this is Ireland? Also, I had a root around the park and I found my bicycle. So a good day overall.

## BEYOND OLÉ OLÉ - GREAT TRUE WORLD CUP FACTS

A BBC World Service report has claimed that, when Nigeria were knocked out of the 1994 World Cup, their Government insisted on having a Welcome Home celebration for the team to divert attention away from the political and economic crisis Nigeria is going through. No further comment necded.

Not a good week for the semi-state sector. More Dreamer Lingus staff were laid off yesterday. The Irish Steal workers will vote on Monday on whether or not they want to keep their jobs. So naturally the weekend papers were filled with speculation on the increasingly tense jobs crisis – emotion-filled photographs, page after page of analysis and opinions: "Should Big Jack Go Now ? " " Will Big Jack stay on ? "

> ## Ninety per cent of the politicians give the other ten per cent a bad reputation

*- Henry Kissinger*

*( ... continued from previous left hand page )*

.... And the first golfer says, "No, actually, I lost". And his friend says "But how ? After all, he only had two gotchas over eighteen holes." And the first golfer says "Have you ever played seventeen holes of golf waiting for a second gotcha ? "

**July 11: On This Day**

Ballyhaunis v New York slagging match enters fifth week, 1987

Lump of coal eaten by unruly child for first time, 1865

## Ten million pound cannibis haul seized off coast

## OJ Simpson pleads not guilty in new tv drama

**July 13: On This Day**

St Francis - look at him there, talking to the sheep and having a bit of a laugh

The Gardai today seized £10 million worth of cannabis off the Connemara coast. They believe it may have taken a wrong turn on its way to the Teagasc research centre in Carlow to make teabags. And the Irish Steal workers voted against keeping their jobs today, so that's the Euro-Piggybank money that little bit safer. Also today, in America, O.J. Simpson went to court, prompting me to pen the following ditty:

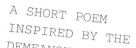

A SHORT POEM INSPIRED BY THE DEMEANOUR AND GENERAL CONFIDENCE OF O.J. SIMPSON IN COURT, WHILE PLEADING "ABSOLUTELY ONE HUNDRED PER CENT NOT GUILTY" TO THE CHARGES AGAINST HIM

ODE TO O.J.'S INNOCENT PLEA

© John Mackay 1994

He looks and sounds
So calm and cool –
The credibility factor

He's either innocent or else
a bloody brilliant actor

Dreamer Lingus today laid off some more workers today, but our overall plan isn't working. We heard today from Bruce Millan (who is not related to the millans and millans that ~~Gerry~~ Gerard Collins is always talking about) that our European Piggybank allocation is still down by a few hundred millan (which _is_ related to the millans and millans that ~~Gerry~~ Gerard Collins is always talking about) – so we've really got to start closing down some companies fairly soon.

" **I can't say I have met any homosexuals** "

*- Bertie Ahern*

<u>John Mackay's</u>
<u>"Things Not To Say"</u> -
(No. 26 in a series)

Things Not To Say To
The Reverend Ian
Paisley when He Asks
For Suggestions For A
Title For A New TV
Game Show:

"Dublin Or Nothing"

6 billion

### July 14: On This Day
Good day for shopping
Agriculture invented, 15 b.c.

## Germany wins World Cup with win over Italy

### July 17: Diary Entry
"Arrived in Ireland. Will try to make most of my visit by converting the locals to Christianity and getting rid of the snakes. Told one of my captors about God sending down His only Son to die on the Cross in order to save mankind, and he thought I was mad. Admittedly it sounds a bit far fetched when you tell it like that to somebody for the first time. However, one of his mates said he was getting a bit disillusioned with Paganism and was interested in getting 'into something new'. I'll try to get chatting to him again tomorrow."

*Saint Patrick*
*July 17, 1415*

Niamh Bhrassneck had another row about sex education with the local school committee today. They asked her does she know what the word "f * * k" means, and when she said yes, they told her to f * * k off then. Sure what can she expect trying to get people involved in education to do any work over the summer? And come to think of it, isn't she meant to be on holidays herself? She'll get us all a bad name. I'll have to talk to her (after the holidays)

## STRANGE TALES OF ORDINARY GARDENING FOLK

Austin Deasy this week called on people with their own back gardens to grow their own vegetables as they would be "performing a patriotic act". The host of the new RTE Gardening Show, "Adams Apple", later said this explains why so many members of the Republican movement spend their time digging in fields late at night.

I got a bit of a shock when I turned on the telly this evening. Even though the World Cup ended two weeks ago when we lost to Holland, it seems that they've simply been carrying on anyway without us. They had the final today. It was between Italy, who I thought we had knocked out in our first match, and Brazil, who beat them 0-0, just like our 0-0 win against Romania four years ago. So its all over now. A funny old game.

**Outside of the killings, we have one of the lowest crime rates in the country**

*- Marion Barry, Mayor of Washington*

John Mackay's Law Of Privatised Nepotism

(No. 1 in a series)

A man who can afford to employ his own children is as well off as if he actually was a Government Minister

**July 18: On This Day**

Fianna Fail Council lifts ban on artificial hares at Thurles greyhound races, 1956

Mullingar cleric fails drug test after Dublin mini-marathon sack race ends in controversy, 1980

**63 year old has child by Artificial Insemnation**

**July 20: On This Day**

Fianna Fail Council lifts ban on artificial greyhounds at Thurles greyhound races, 1957

Coins used as money for the first time, 11 b.c.

I went over to Brussels this week to have a word with some of our M.E.P.s about voting for Jack Santy Claus as the new President of the Piggybank. We went for a nice meal in the Piggybank restaurant, where we met the manager. "Bon apetit", he said, introducing himself. "John Mackay" I replied, shaking his hand. A very nice man, Mr Apetit. And then the waiter introduced himself. It seems his name is Bon Apetit as well. They must all sound the same, as well as looking the same.

~~Gerry~~ Gerard Collins - who knows a lot about foreign restaurants - told me today that "bon apetit" means "enjoy your meal". Crap. Total crap. Why didn't someone tell me? Before dinner today, I approached the manager and said "Bon Apetit". He replied "John Mackay" and shook my hand. I'm totally lost now. At least tomorrow I'll be back home in Ireland, where we all speak English.

### VATICAN NEWSFLASH

The Vatican today condemned the Artificial Insemination of a sixty three year old woman because "the means by which her desire was realised is in open contrast to God's plan." The Pope then went indoors to exercise his new artificial hip. He later ordered a new artificial heart when he saw the wedding photos of the Cranberries' Dolores O'Riordan in the newspapers.

> **The Sunday Independent's highly paid bootboy**

*- Eamon Dunphy on himself*

**July 21: On This Day**

Tralee debating competition won by stork, 1988

Ratio of clouds to people in Mullaghmore "a major public concern" says report, 1967

John Mackay's "Things Not To Say" – (No. 27 in a series)

Things Not To Say To Alan Dukes When Waiting On Him at a Restaurant:

"Your soup, sir. And which fork would you like?"

## Beef Tribunal report to be published soon

## Tension between Fianna Fail and Labour

**July 24: On This Day**

Wrap up well

Cold for this time of year

6 billion

We heard today that the Final Report of the Bunburger Tribunal may be ready next week. This is likely to cause no end of trouble, and is a large part of the reason why Dickie Mandate used to say such nasty things about me. What happened was this: four years ago, a local businessman by the name of Larry Goodmanyourself opened a chipper, and asked us to help him subsidise buying bunburgers from the local butchers in Emerald Meadows. Then Dessie Candoit discovered that what

Goodmanyourself was actually buying was leftovers from the bins round the back of the local MacBurger Multinational Fast Food Emporium. Of course, I knew nothing about this, as you can only get so much information onto one page. But everyone else went mad about it, particularly the Progressive Detectives, so we agreed to set up a Tribunal to adjudicate. And now the sky is dark with flocks of cattle coming home to roost.

A SHORT POEM INSPIRED BY THE DANGERS AND THE PARADOXICAL BENEFITS OF BEING IN A POSITION OF RESPONSIBILITY WHEN DECISIONS HAVE TO BE MADE WITH CONSEQUENCES OF AN UNPREDICTABLE NATURE

ODE TO AN UNLUCKY BET

© John Mackay 1994

I'm not irrational, just unlucky -
Bet on National Interest. Fuck, he
lost the race, but it's still funny
It was someone else's money

> **If God had been a liberal, we would have had the Ten Suggestions**

*- Malcolm Bradbury and Christopher Brigsby*

Wednesday July 27:
He's back! Gumshoe McDuel has discovered that my family may benefit from a Tidy Town grant that C.R.A.P. has offered to some residents, and he has optimistically asked DICKIE MANDATE to investigate it! (the words "poacher" and "gamekeeper" immediately spring to mind)

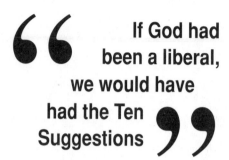

6 billion

**July 25: Diary Entry**

"Everything here reeks of value. The competitively priced babies' disposable nappies; the sausages; the beautifully packaged sanitary products. Even the toilet paper appears strangely beautiful - as well, of course, as having tremendous value. As I walk around the store this morning, I imagine our rivals seething with jealousy - slitting their wrists with rage, their blood oozing onto their inferior shoddily packaged tea bags and cans of dogfood. Ha! Ha! Ha!"

*Maurice Pratt*
*January 25 1997*

## McDowell wants Longford zoning plan examined

**July 27: On This Day**

Pencil parers rapped by Bishop on Late Late Show 'Pencils Special', 1973

Entire population of Leitrim emigrates to America, 1879

# The Great Ballinasloe Bike Robbery

### In what year was the following question asked in the Dáil?

> To ask the Minister for Defence whether he is aware that members of the National Forces in Ballinasloe have gone around the town on two or three occasions and taken up all the bicycles they could find, without stating the purpose of such seizure, and whether he will have full enquiries made into this complaint and have the bicycles returned.

## Who was the Minister and what reply did he give?

**Reply (a)**

Our Defence Forces are supplied with official motorised transportation. However, due to a combination of unusually heavy rain and the frankly abysmal state of the roads in Ballinasloe, the temporary use of non-Government-issued transport was deemed necessary.

**Reply (b)**

I am aware that bicycles have been commandeered by our troops in Ballinasloe. They were taken and are being retained as a matter of military necessity to facilitate the rounding up of Irregulars, for which purpose they have been very successfully used.

**Reply (c)**

The Deputy knows full well that it is irresponsible to wheel out such a charge without corroboratory evidence. I must furthermore put on record that the Deputy's statement at this sensitive time could be construed as pedalling treason.

Answers: 1922; reply (b) - and the Minister was General Mulcahy

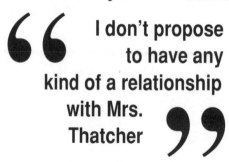

**I don't propose
to have any
kind of a relationship
with Mrs.
Thatcher**

*- Charles J. Haughey*

John Mackay's
"Things Not To Say" -
(No. 28 in a series)

Things Not To Say To
Terry Prone:

"But is it not true
that appearances
only _appear_ to be
important?"

**July 28: On This Day**

Holy Day of Obligation

You *have* to go to Mass - even if you
don't want to

# Beef tribunal report given to government

# Reynolds "totally vindicated" by Tribunal report

**July 30: On This Day**

Average height in Achill 'medium'
states report, 1976

W.T. Cosgrave hissed at by man in
crowd unhappy with Civil War
outcome, 1924

6 billion

**Thursday 28**

At today's C.R.A.P. Committee meeting, we agreed
that none of us would say anything about the Bunburger Tribunal
Report until we all had a chance to discuss it at next week's
meeting. And everybody seemed happy enough with that. Indeed,
as Dympna pointed out over dinner, if Dickie had trusted me four
years ago as much as he does today, there would have been no
need for the Tribunal in the first place!

**Friday 29**

Got to bed very late tonight. We finally
got the first copy of the Bunburger
Tribunal Report, so I got
Diggy to go
dotty with
an urgent
press release.

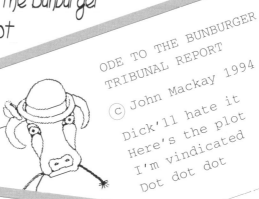

ODE TO THE BUNBURGER
TRIBUNAL REPORT

© John Mackay 1994

Dick'll hate it
Here's the plot
I'm vindicated
Dot dot dot

**CRAP** URGENT PRESS RELEASE

ISSUED 2.30 A.M.
OFFICIAL EXTRACTS FROM
BUNBURGER TRIBUNAL REPORT

1. "The decision was a matter for ... Mr
   Mackay, who is clearly ... innocent
   ... and should in all probability get
   ... a large pay rise."

2. "Furthermore, Mr Mackay ... is in all
   likelihood ... God."

**August 1: On This Day**

St Dominic's Day of Shame

Thunder and lightning linked together for first time by scientists, 1567

" **When the President does it, that means it's not illegal** "

*- Richard Nixon*

John Mackay's Anthology Of Really Crap Jokes I Heard In The Pub This Year:

(No. 9 in a series)

Two couples, both on their honeymoons, get a bit tipsy and decide to swap partners for a night of illicit passion. The next morning, one husband says to the other "last night was great." And the other husband says "Yeah, I agree. I wonder how the women got on?"

Opposition query Reynolds claim of "vindication"

**August 2: On This Day**

A daisy a day

**August 3: On This Day**

Van Morrison leaps over tall building to publicise new album, 1970

Enniscorthy blown away in gale, 1778

6 billion

**Monday 1**

DID SOME RESEARCH IN THE LIBRARY TODAY ON THE
IRISH LANGUAGE. IT'S FUNNY HOW THE IRISH WORDS
FOR THINGS THAT DIDN'T EXIST IN OLDEN TIMES ARE
QUITE RECOGNISABLE.

| | |
|---|---|
| An disco | The disco |
| An aerphort | The airport |
| An stáisiún traenach | The train station |
| An tótal agus absolút waste of feicin money | The tribunal |

**[...]ay 2**

As I expected, Dickie's tantrum
is over, having called me a policy disaster (I've been called worse).
However, he is still in a sulk, and isn't speaking to me. And the
Progressive Detectives and Run Rabbitte Run have been complaining
about the gaps in the extracts that I made public (it was only a
few pages). I told them that they would see the full report, like
everyone else, when we publish it on ..... or no later than .........

**Wednesday 3**

Young Suzie has read the whole report and she told
me today that, in her opinion, it concluded that I was not corrupt,
just incompetent. And now they're all going on as if it was corrupt
to be incompetent! That's crap, total crap. I may be incompetent,
but I'm not stupid. And Big Tim Commie is going on about the Red
Rose lot withdrawing from the C.R.A.P. Committee, even though he's
not on it himself. Who does he think he is, Gumshoe McDuel?

**" He rings up Des
O'Malley in my
presence and says
"hello Des, this is Charlie
Haughey. Did I send
you a Christmas Card?"
And Dessie is in his
office wondering what
all this is about. So he
said "you didn't actually".
So he just went
berserk "**

*- Mary Harney on
Charles J. Haughey's
Christmas Card list*

### John Mackay's Law
### Of Cause And Effect

(No. 2 in a series)

Most politicians are
caused by voters

6 billion

**August 4: On This Day**

Oliver J. Flanagan emits roar that can
be heard ten miles away after seeing
Boomtown Rats on television, 1978

GAA lift ban on suicide at Railway Cup
finals, 1970

**August 5: On This Day**

What a difference a day makes
Except this one - who'd miss it?

Goodman group
to qualify for
Tax Amnesty?

**August 7: On This Day**

Nuclear bomb washed up on Kerry
coast, 1956

### Thursday 4

Dickie had another mini-tantrum today. He was being interviewed on C.R.A.P. FM this morning about his assertion that I was a policy disaster, and he came up with a great new strategy for dealing with awkward questions. You just ignore the question entirely and say nothing, so the interviewer eventually has to ask you if you are still there, then while he's still confused by that you say "I haven't changed from my position" but you refuse to say which of your positions you haven't changed from.

### Friday 5

More bunburger fuss. The report found that Larry Goodmanyourself hadn't paid all of his membership fees to the Residents Association, and now the whingers are complaining that he may be availing of our late membership fee amnesty scheme. Are they never happy? The way they're going on, you'd think he'd committed a crime. Makes you think, though – if he won't settle his fees, will he pay his dues?

A SHORT POEM TO CELEBRATE THE FACT THAT, AFTER A TRAUMATIC AND SENSITIVE STAGE IN OUR PARTNERSHIP, DICKIE'S CHILDISH TANTRUMS ARE OVER AND WE'RE ALL TALKING TO ONE ANOTHER AGAIN

ODE TO FAIR PLAY IN THE BEEF INDUSTRY

© John Mackay 1994

Dickie had a plan today
He wanted us to try
A Beef Monopolies Commission
"What, only one?" said I

**August 8: On This Day**

Easi-Singles "an innovation in the cheese industry which can only lead to chaos and a breakdown of the family as we know it" says Bishop of Down and Conor, 1970

" **If a tree fell in a forest, and no-one was there to hear it, it might sound like Dan Quayle looks** "

*- Tom Shales*

John Mackay's
"Things Not To Say" -
(No. 29 in a series)

Things Not To Say To Ivan Yates Before A Dáil Debate On Tax:

" here's a hint, Ivan. I know it can be tricky to remember *all* the rules, but ... when we decide on a policy, *we* support it, and *they* oppose it "

## Team Aer Lingus workers disrupt airport traffic

## O'Sullivan wins gold at European Championship

**August 10: On This Day**

Sand used on beaches for first time, 1889

6 billion

**Monday 8**

The Dreamer Lingus pickets today blocked the main road outside the airport, disrupting traffic and delaying flights. Now, I know we need to close down some businesses to make sure we still qualify for our Euro-Piggybank money, but we don't want people's holiday plans upset – especially our own. Riffo Cowen was particularly angry. He's never been a socialist anyway, and today he was pacing up and down all day humming "You've got to sock a picket or two".

**Tuesday 9**

## THE PADDY COX HA HA HA GUIDE TO GREAT POLICEMEN OF OUR TIME

1. Merciless Bastard of Dock Green
2. Hill Street Bastards
3. The very nice Gardai who stopped the Dreamer Lingus pickets from disrupting the destiny of people like me who fly a lot

**...ay 10**

More Dreamer Lingus disruptions today – but some good news as well. Sonia O'Sullivan won a gold medal in the European Championships – a first for the country! The whole family is looking forward to the big Welcome Home Open-Air Disco in the Phoenix Park. And this time it'll be an even bigger celebration than the soccer one, with even bigger bands and even more saturation television coverage, as Sonia actually won!

" **I hate people who can't decide what to eat for breakfast until they find out what Trotsky had in 1917** "

*- Roddy Doyle*

John Mackay's
"Things Not To Say" -

(No. 30 in a series)

Things Not To Say To Jim Kemmy:

"You know what I really used to hate when the PDs were in Coalition? The way Michael McDowell used to use his position as Party Chairman to publicly slag off his own government"

6 billion

**August 11: Diary Entry**

"I MET A MAN TODAY AND HE SAID TO ME "THEY DON'T CALL YOU 'BIG IAN' FOR NOTHING". "NO", I SAID! "THE REASON THEY CALL ME 'BIG IAN' IS THAT I AM BIG!" I THOUGHT ABOUT HOW BIG I AM FOR THE REST OF THE DAY! IT'S NOTICEABLE THAT NO ONE GOES AROUND CALLING JOHN HUME 'BIG JOHN'! OR WEE JIMMY MOLYNEAUX 'BIG JIMMY MOLYNEAUX'! NO! NOW THERE'S SOMETHING FOR ALBERT REYNOLDS AND JOHN MAJOR AND THE REST OF THEM TO THINK ABOUT AS THEY SELL THE PEOPLE OF ULSTER UP THE SWANEE AND DOWN THE DUBLIN ROAD!"

*Rev Ian Paisley*
*August 11 1998*

# Archbishop upset at media focus on Bishop Casey

**July 27: On This Day**

Bendable paper introduced, 1900

The whole family went down to the Park today for Sonia O'Sullivan's Welcome Home Open-Air Disco, but it must have been over by the time we got there. In fact, they'd already taken the stage down again (of course, they've had a lot of practice at that) and the park was completely deserted except for the usual gang of cyclists, Government Ministers and merciless bastards.

## AMAZING BUT TRUE REAL-LIFE ANNOUNCEMENTS AT PUBLIC EVENTS No. 763

Tolka Park, Dublin, Sat Aug 13, just before the Shelbourne v Leeds match: "Ladies and gentlemen, in front of the main stand, in recognition of his performance in the World Cup, our sponsors SDS will now present a glass thing to Gary Kelly."

## VATICAN NEWSFLASH

The Archbishop of Dublin today gave a major interview to a Sunday paper, in which he complained about all of the media publicity given to Bishop Casey. You know the sort of thing - journalists reminding people of the scandal whenever Bishop Casey says Mass or goes to a football match, and Archbishops reminding people of the scandal in newspaper interviews.

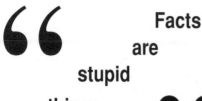

**" Facts
are
stupid
things "**

*- Ronald Reagan,
misquoting John Quincy
Adams' more plausible
assertion that "facts are
stubborn things"*

John Mackay's
"Things Not To Say" -
(No. 31 in a series)

Things Not To Say To
John Bruton When he
Makes a Mistake:

" You just can't open
your mouth without
putting your children's
shoes in it, can you ? "

**August 15: On This Day**

Women allowed to become half of
married couple for first time, 1770

Animal wigs "unnecessary" states
Bishop of Cashel in 'we are all God's
creatures' speech, 1958

**Team Aer Lingus
traffic disruptions
continue**

**August 17: On This Day**

United Nations recognise Nigeria after
thinking it was somebody else, 1966

Sickly cow wins first all-animal Grand
National, 1889

## LATEST NEWSFLASH

There was serious disruption today at Dublin Airport, where the Dreamer Lingus workers conducted a road blockage for several hours. They then wheel-clamped some of the cars they delayed, seized and ate the ignition keys from others, then threw stinkbombs into the cars and superglued the windows shut. "We don't want to inconvenience the public" said a union spokesperson, "But what else can we do?"

16

Bertie Bucks told me today that one of President Clinton's top officials had been forced to resign, and I said why, and Bertie said because he had misled their parliament, and I said, no, I mean, why did he have to resign, and Bertie said because he misled their parliament, and I said he had to RESIGN because he misled their parliament, and Bertie said yes, and I said HA HA HA HA HA HA !!!!!!!!

## LATEST NEWSFLASH

Disruptions continued today at Dublin Airport. After today's ignition-key seizures, the workers left all the courtesy telephones in the airport off the hook after dialling the talking clock in Australia. They then hijacked three incoming airplanes and held the passengers hostage until after the last bus into town had left. "We don't want to inconvenience the public" said a union spokesperson, "But what else can we do?"

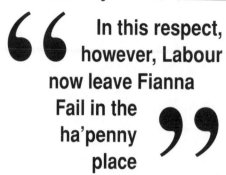

**In this respect, however, Labour now leave Fianna Fail in the ha'penny place**

*- Sean Haughey
on powerlust*

*John Mackay's Law Of The Immutable Inter-Relationship Between Time, Power, Money and Bags*

*(No. 3 in a series)*

*The average time between Fianna Fail losing an election and returning to power is inversely proportional to the amount of billions of Euro-money claimed to be in the bag*

**August 18: On This Day**

Not *quite* a full moon - one of those ones where a bit of the edge is slightly blurred

Vatican bookies declare bankruptcy as Pope Buckley the first is enthroned, 1995

Centenary of 1798 rebellion, 1898

**Team Aer Lingus traffic disruptions continue**

**August 21: On This Day**

Loophole which allows murder and robbery in Finglas finally closed after long legal battle, 1979

Fish develop gills, 55 b.c.

Sonia O'Sullivan yesterday narrowly failed to break
the world mile record, and a thought struck Dympna - maybe the
huge crowd for the soccer team was because they had lost
instead of won. So we all went down to the Phoenix Park for the
Sonia O'Sullivan Welcome Home Open-Air Commiserations Disco. Alas!
Like last week, we again got there too late, the event was
over and everyone had gone home. Maybe next time.

**DREAMER LINGUS**

## LATEST NEWSFLASH

Disruptions continued today at Dublin
Airport. After hijacking three airplanes,
the Dreamer Lingus workers seized a
ninety seven year old passenger and burned
her flight ticket, then marched her down to a
local park where they covered her with honey and
buried her up to her neck beside an ant-hill.
"We don't want to inconvenience the public" said a
union spokesperson, "But what else can we do?"

I couldn't think of anything to write
today, so I asked Dympna if she had any ideas. She
suggested writing an entry about the fact that I couldn't think of
anything to write today, but I said, don't be daft, sure that would
only take up one line, and she said, not if you pad it out a bit by
saying that you asked me for any ideas and that I suggested
that you pad it out a bit, and I said, nah, it would never work.

❝ **If you don't want to work for a living, this is as good a job as any** ❞

*- John F. Kennedy*

<u>John Mackay's Anthology Of Really Crap Jokes I Heard In The Pub This Year:</u>

(No. 10 in a series)

What do you say to a politician who has just been promoted to a more important job?

"a big mac, large fries and a regular coke, please"

5 billion

**August 22: On This Day**

No stone left unturned in Wicklow Stone Turning Competition, 1967

Brendan Bowyer's voice breaks, 1952

## The General is shot dead outside his home

**August 23: On This Day**

First Tuesday of the week

**August 24: On This Day**

The joys of hill climbing discovered, 1756

Rome built in a day, 56 b.c.

## QUE SERA SERA - SEVEN REASONS WHY THE GENERAL SHOULD BE ROMANTICISED

1. He made it easier for the Gardai to play golf by widening the holes when he dug up the greens on their golf course

2. He helped the economy by increasing newspaper sales and boosting the demand for new unslashed car tyres

3. He was the only person in the world to violate the Walt Disney Mickey Mouse copyright and not get sued for it

4. He gave valuable driving practice to detectives tailing him in unmarked police cars, by going to a roundabout and driving round it forty times

5. He gave new meaning to the concept of maintaining the family as the basic unit of Irish society

6. When in custody he always got what he wanted by asking for the opposite (i.e. if he wanted the lights out he would insist they stay on, and vice versa)

7. He only ever nailed anybody to the floor if it was absolutely necessary

> ❝ **We are in an era of time when self-control seems to have been put aside as a value** ❞

*Bishop Eamon Casey*

*John Mackay's Law Of The Type Of Public Relations Policy That We All Know Charlie McCreevy Would Never Tolerate:*

*(No. 4 in a series)*

*It is not so much a question of being right, but of having better explanations for being wrong*

**August 25: Diary Entry**

"I was shot dead today. Wow! I was driving along a road in west Cork when our convoy was ambushed. I jumped out in the middle of the road to have a pot at some of them when a bullet hit me in the head. That obviously puts an end to my fight for Irish freedom. I asked God what is going to happen to Ireland and I got some answer which mentioned something called the Eurovision Song Contest. What does that mean? Who knows! Heaven looks very like Roscommon, incidentally."

*Michael Collins*
*August 22, 1922*

## GAA introduce new logo "to make money"

## DPP orders arrest of Beef Tribunal journalist

**August 27: On This Day**

Sun up. Arise. Sun down. Go to bed.

**Thursday 25**

The G.A.A. today launched their new logo. It's designed like one of those ink-blob tests that psychoanalysts use, and if you look at it at a certain angle with your eyes half closed, you can see a Union Jack being burned while an R.U.C. man is being sent off a G.A.A. pitch by a referee with a large hurley. The G.A.A. say it is aimed at making more money, as they had legal problems copyrighting the old one, so presumably they've finally decided to go for drinks sponsorship as you'd have to have a fair few pints on you before you could even start to understand the new logo.

**Friday 26**

The Bunburger Tribunal today claimed its first victim, with the Director of Public Prosecutions ordering the arrest of the notorious criminal Susan "Supergrass" O'Keefe. The reason for the decision was later explained at a Press Conference: "This is a clear message to the public and politicians alike that the courts simply will not tolerate wrongdoing on the scale of that exposed by this Tribunal" said an ass.

JOHN MACKAY'S "THINGS NOT TO SAY" ALL TIME HALL OF FAME CLASSIC

Things Not To Say When Arresting Susan O'Keefe:

" You have the right to remain silent ..."

**August 29: On This Day**

Pins invented, 1266

Needles invented, 1267

" **They are going around the country stirring up complacency** "

*- Willie Whitelaw on the British Labour Party in Government*

Beef Tribunal debate scheduled for Wednesday

John Mackay's "Things Not To Say" -

(No. 32 in a series)

Things Not To Say To Sinn Fein If You Are John Major:

Anything

IRA announces total cessation of military activities

**August 31: On This Day**

Nails invented, 1268

Invention of hammer "still some time away" states nail inventor, 1269

5 billion

We had a bit of a problem today, but we sorted it out in the end. We were about to start the C.R.A.P. debate on the Bunburger Tribunal Report, and neither Dickie nor I were looking forward to the grilling ahead of us. Then we had a brainwave! Why not see if we can do something mad to overshadow the proceedings? So we checked with Johnny Foregreenfield and he said that he was close to convincing his mad Uncle Gerry to stop annoying people in the Norn Iron Shipyard. Don't be

daft, we said, sure that dispute has been going on for a quarter of a century, it's nearly as intractable as Dreamer Lingus. Ah, no, said Johnny, sure mad uncle Gerry's mad altogether, he'll probably stop if you agree to shake hands with him. (Well, to be honest, he said something unintelligible about the need to transcend the relationship between the traditional consent of the three sets of allegiences, but in the end it all seemed to come down to shaking hands with mad uncle Gerry, so we said okay, then)

**Wednesday 31**

HOLD THE FRONT PAGE & DIG OUT THE BIGGEST TYPEFACE HEADING YOU CAN FIND - IT'S "PEACE IN OUR TIME" TIME !

THE IRA TODAY ANNOUNCED A COMPLETE CESSATION OF MILITARY ACTIVITIES, BUT CONTINUED TO ORDER JOYRIDERS AND PETTY CRIMINALS OUT OF BELFAST. A SPOKESMAN EXPLAINED THIS WAS IN LINE WITH THEIR NEW POLICY SLOGAN "TIME FOR PEACE - TIME TO GO"

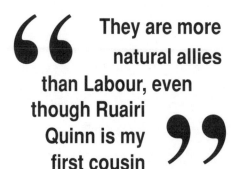

**They are more natural allies than Labour, even though Ruairi Quinn is my first cousin**

*- Brendan McGahon on the Progressive Democrats*

**September 1: On This Day**

Feast of Some Souls (the bigger ones)

Enniscorthy blown away in gale, 1778

_John Mackay's Law Of The Only Certain Way Of Solving The Problems Of Unemployment, Taxation And The National Debt :_

(No. 5 in a series)

Only the opposition knows how to do this

Reynolds brings an end to 800 years of conflict

Reynolds "unfit for public office", says Bruton

**September 3: On This Day**

Sheep-to-people ratio in Mullingar becomes 12:1, 1988

**Thursday 1**

This ceasefire is truly historic. Already it has completely transformed the political situation beyond recognition - the Bunburger Tribunal debate has been rescheduled, nobody gives a damn about it any more anyway, and - while everyone is in such a good mood - we've also sneaked in a small seventeen percent pay rise for myself and Dickie Mandate !!!! (Honestly, I don't know why we didn't think of shaking hands with mad uncle Gerry long ago.) And West Belfast is mad, mad, mad !!!! I was trying to explain it to Dickie Mandate - the street celebrations,

**Friday 2**

the tricolours, the tooting car horns, the singing and chanting - and the best comparison I could come up with was that it was like the Irish soccer team coming home after the World Cup. Yes, but what exactly are they celebrating, asked Dickie; what exactly have they won ? And I said, well, like I was saying, it's like the Irish soccer team coming home after the World Cup ....

Above: a fax from Ladi Di

## PRINCESS DI IN ANONYMOUS PHONE CALL ALLEGATIONS

Buckingham Palace revealed today that there is an innocent explanation to the allegations that Princess Diana has been making nuisance anonymous telephone calls. Apparently Lady Di had been in Madame Tussauds, and had thought that the wax dummy of herself was too ugly. When she knocked it over and broke it, a tabloid journalist misheard a policeman cautioning her for making an obscene clone fall.

**66** **Because
he uses
too big
a words** **99**

*- Ronald Reagan, on why
he doesn't often quote a
particular author*

John Mackay's
"Things Not To Say" -

(No. 33 in a series)

Things Not To Say To
Gay Or Jim Mitchell
After They Die:

"I'm sorry, Mr
Mitchell, this is Hell.
There <u>are</u> no
facilities for issuing
press releases"

**September 5: On This Day**

Clare man summonsed over "what's
so special about the Special
Olympics?" remark, 1987

Painting becomes an art form, 1499

## Clinton interrupts
## holiday to meet
## Dick Spring

## Cullen defects
## from PDs to join
## Fianna Fail

**September 7: On This Day**

Oliver J Flanagan revealed as
werewolf during Dail debate, 1967

### FIVE THINGS WE CAN EXPECT DICKIE MANDATE NOT TO DO AFTER HIS CASUAL OPEN-SHIRT MEETING WITH BILL CLINTON

1. Hold press conferences on the run while jogging through the Phoenix Park in a tracksuit

2. Develop a reputation for consistently changing his mind about everything

3. Eat loads of hamburgers and chips and smoke cannabis without inhaling

4. Get involved in bizarre controversies over alleged extra-marital affairs

5. Get hammered in the next election

There's always fun and laughs these days down at the Progressive Detective Agency. Today Martin Culumbo resigned, less than four **Wednesday 7** months after Paddy Cox ha ha ha privatised himself.
It seems that Culumbo was upset because Mary Harmony was insisting that he take his turn at washing up the dishes after lunch meetings and ironing his own suit before press conferences. Don't worry, I told him over a pint (now that's a good man's drink), sure that's women for you, and he cheered up immediately and said he'd move in with us at Emerald Meadows.

" I'll bring the whole fucking thing down from the inside "

*- Liam Skelly*

<u>John Mackay's Law Of Political Reputations And The Magic Number Four Hundred And Seventy Nine:</u>

(No. 6 in a series)

It takes four hundred and seventy nine times more effort to turn a bad political reputation into a good one than it does to turn a good political reputation into a bad one

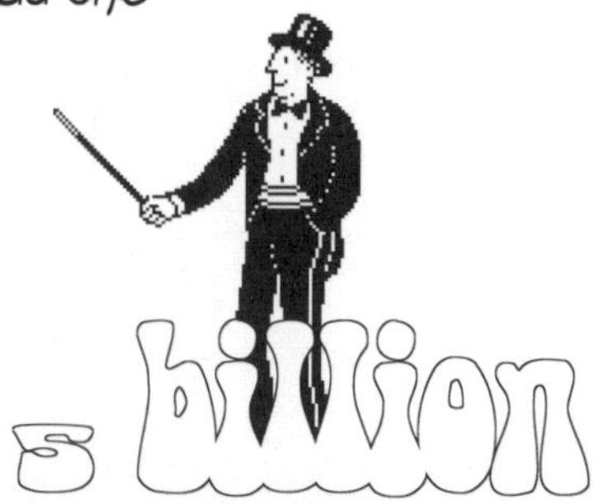

8 billion

**September 8: On This Day**

Second juggler hacked to death in Trim within a week, 1975

Storm blows Inisboffin further away from Irish coast, 1954

# Reynold, Adams, Hume in historic handshake

# Spring fails to Show for historic handshake

**September 11: On This Day**

End of the world?

Probably not.

I've been wrong before.

I sorted out that handshake yesterday with Johnny Foregreenfield and uncle Gerry. It's amazing how wrong you can be about people! Here we've been for twenty odd years thinking uncle Gerry was mad and all the time he was beavering away, like a Mother Teresa with a balaclava instead of tea-towel on his head, to bring about peace to all of his brothers and sisters (including the poor deluded ones who mistakenly believe they aren't members of his family at all and who go all sulky when you fire a few rifle shots at them). I shouted inside for Dickie Mandate to come out and join in the photos (he normally likes that, and will often stand behind me looking over my shoulder when I am being photographed over in England), but surprisingly he didn't come out. I later heard he had gone to Germany to meet a man about a GATT. Perhaps he had forgotten that uncle Gerry was calling today. That must be it. But the whole thing got me thinking – why stop at home, I'll do a world tour and bring peace to all mankind!

A SHORT POEM INSPIRED BY THE SUDDEN AND BLINDING FLASH OF REALISATION THAT I FINALLY UNDERSTAND WHAT JOHN HUME MEANS WHEN HE TALKS ABOUT THE THREE SETS OF RELATIONSHIPS

THE THREE SETS OF RELATIONSHIPS

© John Mackay 1994

We must first define the problem
we all know, I assume,
there's three sets of relationships
Ireland, Britain and John Hume

" **Just put in some of that vision thing** "

*- George Bush instructing a new speech writer*

<u>John Mackay's Anthology Of Really Crap Jokes I Heard In The Pub This Year</u>:

(No. 11 in a series)

A film director was making an epic about Noah, when he discovered that some of the animals were multiplying on the ark. So he became the first biblical director to have bred his cast upon the waters.

**September 12: Diary Entry**

"Sat beside the Irish Prime Minister at summit meeting in Brussels. A fellow with strange frizzy hair. We also ended up beside each other at dinner. I noticed that during the coffee he was scribbling on a serviette for some reason. He noticed that I had been watching this and seemed embarrassed. Immediately he tried to interest me in a discussion about Northern Ireland, a topic I have absolutely no interest in. When he went to the bathroom I took a closer look at the serviette and saw that he had jotted down a lot of figures which he seemed to have been adding and subtracting from each other. As he came back, he tripped over President Mitterand and fell into the fire. His frizzy hair was ablaze for several seconds, much to the amusement of the other heads of State. What an unusual man."

*Margaret Thatcher, September 12 1987*

Craftworkers refuse Irish Steel rescue deal

# CRAP

## the Combined Residents Association Partnership

between Emerald Meadows and the Red Rose Corporation Estate

Minutes of C.R.A.P. meeting, September 1994

1. Everyone congratulated the Chairman, Mr Mackay, on bringing peace to the neighbourhood after 800 years of conflict and wished him well on his forthcoming world tour aimed at bringing peace and harmony to all of mankind.

2. Treasurer's Report:
   Mr Bertie Bucks impressed on everybody the urgency of closing down Dreamer Lingus and Irish Steal, as our economic performance is now dangerously close to being too good to qualify for the same amount of European Piggybank Money next time around.

   Mr Riffo Cowen explained that things were going quite well at Dreamer Lingus - as planned, the workers were still disrupting traffic and it shouldn't be long before the public completely (and permanently) lose sympathy with them.

   Mr Ruari Rua told the Committee that the Irish Steal unions have voted to accept the rescue plan, so it looks like the company will be able to stay in business. The Committee commiserated with Mr Rua, and thanked him for his trojan, though sadly unsuccesful, efforts to have it closed down.

14

*Ruari Rua was in a much better mood today - it seems the Irish Steal Craftworkers have decided to reject the rescue plan after all! So now the management have been able to start laying off workers, and the company should be closed within a week! Great!*

> " I'd get rid of characters like Dick Spring who seem indistinguishable from the average British Tory "

- Ken Livingstone

John Mackay's "Things Not To Say" -

(No. 34 in a series)

Things Not To Say To Charlie Redmond After The 1994 All Ireland Final:

"Here's your new contract, Mr Redmond. As you can see, we've added a penalty clause."

**September 15: On This Day**

Moon made out of cheese

Bathers wishing to use the pool during night time hours do so at their own peril

## Craftworkers dispute intensifies at Irish Steel

## Reynolds visits Hong Kong to start world tour

**September 18: On This Day**

Pig racing deemed "offensive to pigs" in report by clergy, 1972

# THE PSYCHOLOGY OF INTERPERSONAL COMMUNICATION

### LESSON ONE: WHY SPEAKING ENGLISH TO CRAFTWORKERS IN COBH DOESN'T WORK

What you mean to convey: "We have to change how we do things around here or we'll all be on the dole"

What you actually say: "I know you haven't had to do this before, but is there any chance you might be able to move this object from here to over there in this forklift truck?"

What the Craftworker hears: "You good for nothing bastard, I'm going to make you murder your granny and boil her face in a vat of oil"

What the Craftworker means to convey: "No"

What the Craftworker actually says: "No"

What you hear: "No"

I touched down in Hong Kong today on the first leg of the John Mackay 1994 Global Peace and Reconciliation Tour. It seems they've had a few

centuries of a dispute over who owns the place, but I sat them all down together and we sorted it out fairly quickly. What's next? Australia? That won't take long. Although I believe Eoghan Harris is fairly popular there - or is that his brother Rolf? Then on to New Zealand, and back to Shannon to meet that nice Mr Yeltsin from Russia. If I'm quick I might be able to drop in on Bosnia and sort that out on the way home.

> **A billion here, a billion there, and pretty soon you're talking about real money**

*- US Senator Everett Dirksen on fiscal policy*

*John Mackay's Law Of The Psychology Of Crucial Decisions On The Formation Of Coalition Governments*

*(No. 7 in a series)*

*Any decision, however objectively unwise, can be rationalised by the presence of eight, or even six, billion pounds*

**September 19: On This Day**

Sinn Fein Publicity Bureau launch new fundraising extravaganza with unveiling of First Annual Paramilitary Spring and Autumn Fashion Collection, 1995

## Contention over High Court Presidency job

## Liquidator is finally appointed to Irish Steel

**September 21: On This Day**

Feast of very fat people

**Monday 19**

Got a funny phone call today from back home. The Residents Association is entitled to nominate the President of the Neighbourhood Watch Committee, and it seems Dickie Mandate wants some woman or other to get the job. However, I understand there is a constitutional convention that requires the job to go to someone to whom I've already given another job in the past, and I'm not the sort of person to break such a ~~useful~~ longstanding convention. Furthermore, as I think it's the sort of job that can be done by almost anyone, I've already

**Tuesday 20**

offered it to my old mate Tom Dickorharry. Dickie will probably go into another of his silly tantrums but, as they might say over here in China, we'll see a sweet and sour Spring roll when things get too hot for him.

# CRAP

## the Combined Residents Association Partnership
### between Emerald Meadows and the Red Rose Corporation Estate

Minutes of Emergency C.R.A.P. meeting, September 1994

1. In the absence of the Chairman, Mr Mackay, and the vice-chairman, Mr Mandate, a motion was put to nominate Mr Tom Dickorharry as President of the Neighbourhood Watch. So that's that settled, then.

2. Mr Ruari Rua told the Committee that a liquidator had finally been appointed to Irish Steal. Everyone laughed a lot, then a statement was drafted accepting this development "with deep regret".

**All women
will always
be girls**

*- Chris Kirwan*

John Mackay's
"Things Not To Say" -

(No. 35 in a series)

Things Not To Say To John Hume
As An Offer To Finally Settle The
Northern Ireland
Problem:

"Okay, John, you win.
You can have a united
Ireland - but only if
you can tell us why
you want it using
words of less than six
syllables each "

**September 22: Diary Entry**

"Full of ideas for the new flag. I'm
pressing for the idea that there
should be a picture of me in the
middle on the white bit, as green
white and orange is a bit dull. I also
thought that 'Eamon de Valera's
Ireland' sounds better than just
'Ireland' on its own. Anyway, the
main thing is that Fianna Fail are in
power at last! An all Irish speaking
nation within three weeks! Great!"

*Eamon de Valera*
*September 22, 1932*

## Reynolds visits Australia and New Zealand

## Irish Steel craftworkers hold new ballot

## RISE IN NUMBERS SEEKING INTERMEDIARY CERTIFICATE

The number of intermediaries in the Northern Ireland peace process today finally exceeded the number of people who were in the GPO in 1916, when popular children's television star Postman Pat claimed to have been a government intermediary for several years. "Every day I deliver thousands of letters" he explained. "Any one of those could be from the government, perhaps asking Jimmy Saville to solve the Northern Ireland problem on Jim'll Fix It. And if that doesn't make me a government intermediary then I'm The Fat Controller from Thomas The Tank Engine."

Australia today - a place with so many links to home. It was here that the Garda Heavy Gang made a hames of it and said Alderman Nicky Kelly planned the Sallins Train Robbery (they said he planned to disguise himself with a metal bucket over his head, but then they discovered that their forensics expert was confusing Nicky with some other Kelly). Alderman Kelly's pardon, incidentally is only Number 3 on The World's Greatest Ever Reversal Of Anything Top Ten list. Number 2 was the acceptance by the Vatican that Galileo was, how can I put it diplomatically, erm... right. And The World's Number One Greatest Ever Reversal Of Anything is ... (long drum roll) ... The sensational and selfless decision this weekend by our flexible friends, the Irish Steal Craftworkers, that they could, in fact, operate forklift trucks rather than close down the entire town of Cobh.

> " Let each of us ask, not just what will government do for me, but what I can do for myself "

*- Richard Nixon, in his second inaugural address*

John Mackay's Law Of Resolving Conflicts Over Judicial Appointments In The Most Un-Ross-Perot-Like Manner Possible:

(No. 8 in a series)

When in doubt, form a committee

5 billion

**September 26: On This Day**

British peasants agree to lowest minimum wage, 1089

Man evolves from small fish stage after weeks of trying, 3,020,087 b.c.

## Dispute intensifies over top judicial appointment

## Exclusive: Spring and Reynolds to talk by telephone ?

**September 26: On This Day**

Battery hens rob bank near Ennis, 1978

A SHOLT POEM ON THE CONCELN SHOWN BY MY
CHINESE HOSTS ABOUT DICK SPLING TLYING TO
STOP HALLY WHEREHAN GETTING THE HIGH
COULT JOB

UNIVERSAL SUFFLAGE IN CHINA

ⓒ John Mackay 1994

In their funny chinese accents
They asked of Hally's selection
Is it just a cock-up
Or could it be a general erection

27

Still having problems with Dickie Mandate over
giving Tom Dickorharry the top Neighbourhood Watch job. The main
problem being that I can't for the life of me remember who Dickie
Mandate is or what he looks like. It's now been over three weeks
since I saw him, and he seems so insignificant now that I'm a world
statesman on a par with uncle Gerry. In less than a month I've
brought peace to Hong Kong, China, Australia, and New Zealand. I've
advised Billy Clinton on the phone about Haiti. (I

told him there'd always be problems in a country     **Wednesday 28**
where you can get a divorce so easily). And ever
since I realised that I am now a major player on the global stage,
funny thoughts have been entering my mind, - thoughts which I find
myself increasingly unable to resist. As I fly from hot spot to hot
spot smiling more widely every time I land, the words "majority"
and "overall" are never far from the surface of my consciousness.

> **Essentially, it's bad business, bad politics, bad economics**

*- Raymond Crotty on repaying the National Debt*

John Mackay's
"Things Not To Say" -

(No. 36 in a series)

Things Not To Say In Court As a Defence Against a Charge of Forging Postage Stamps:

"Imitation is the most sincere form of philately"

**September 29: Diary Entry**

"Some resistance to my idea of putting picture of yours truly on new flag. Not from within the party of course - as I obviously don't tolerate any criticism from those half-wits - but from the bastard civil servants. Obviously I should try to replace them, but an unusually high number of my people I have discovered to be completely illiterate, and reading and writing skills are sadly necessary to carry on the day-to-day running of the State. Also, plans to have an all Irish speaking country within a month have run into difficulties. Banning English might do the trick; am also looking into the feasibility of prison sentences for Protestants."

*Eamon de Valera*
*September 29, 1932*

**Shannon waits as Yeltsin sleeps off stopover hangover**

**October 1: On This Day**

Enbalming of the Herded Swine

What a day! I have just flown halfway across the world to meet Boris The Red from Moscow. We had everything set up - the red carpet, a nice meal in a posh historic castle, some treble strength vodka flown in specially .. I can tell you, it wasn't cheap (it might have been cheaper to use the local airport, but we were afraid that Boris might be embarrassed by the Dreamer Lingus workers). Anyway, I brought Bertie Bucks and Riffo Cowen down with me to the airport, as I thought they deserved to see me in action in my new role as World Statesman With a Tan. And then we got there. And we waited. And we waited. And eventually someone came out, but it wasn't Boris. I looked at Bertie, but he just shrugged his shoulders. Then Riffo looked up from his "Shannon Briefing" file, and whispered to me, "It's the Deputy Prime Minister". Of course, I thought, and I put out my hand to introduce myself. "Hello again, Dickie" I said, "You know, it's only been a month and I had totally forgotten what you look like."

A SHORT LIMERICK INSPIRED BY BORIS YELTSIN'S OFFICIAL PROTEST AGAINST THE SHANNON STOPOVER

ODE TO THE SHANNON HANGOVER

© John Mackay 1994

At Shannon with faces as red
As the VIP carpet they said
He may be out soon Al
Don't hold a tribunal
He's not quite yet Boris The Dead

" **A leader should not get too far** in front of his troops or he'll get shot in the arse "

*- Senator Joseph Clarke*

John Mackay's Anthology Of Really Crap Jokes I Heard In The Pub This Year:

(No. 12 in a series)

A man is walking down D'Olier Street when it starts to rain, so he goes into the Irish Times office, grabs a few newspapers, and wipes his feet on them. The editor asks him what he is doing, and he says " these are the Times that dry men's soles "

**October 3: On This Day**

Bigotry enshrined in GAA Constitution, 1899

First non-woollen suits of armour introduced, 1145

## Mackay finds his personal runway to Damascus

**October 4: On This Day**

Moon made out of cheese

**October 5: On This Day**

Bathers wishing to use the pool during night time hours do so at their own peril

**Monday 3**

Last Friday was a turning point in my life. Shannon Airport metamorphised into my personal runway to Damascus when a blinding flash of sunlight, reflected from a vodka bottle, threw me for an instant to the ground floor of my belief system. When I came to, my mind was buzzing with all the unfathomable questions of our time: What is life? Is there an afterlife? Are the deity and the cosmos interdependent? How does the dialectic of Plato contrast with the syllogistic inferences of Aristotle? Why can't the BBC accept that the referee was wrong

**Tuesday 4**

to allow Geoff Hurst's second goal against West Germany in the 1966 World Cup final? And why, oh why, oh why, since Dickie Mandate and his mates will put up with anything to stay on the C.R.A.P. Committee, have we been so tolerant about supporting some of the daftest of their daft ideas? I decided to lock myself, like Rene Descartes, into a heated room and prepare a new life philosophy to guide me through times ahead.

Today I started to write my new personal philosophy of life: "A One Page Theory Of Life, The Afterlife, Plato, Aristotle, Geoff Hurst and Dickie Mandate"

So far I have got thus far:

1. I wink, therefore I am
2. Dickie's pink, therefore he's spam
3. I think I think I smell a stink

**What a waste it is to lose one's mind - or not to have a mind. How true that is**

*- J. Danforth Quayle, addressing an organisation whose slogan is "a wasted mind is a terrible thing"*

### October 6: Diary Entry

"Woke up at nine o'clock to discover that I had drunk so much that my left leg had dissolved. Dragged myself out of bed and down to Neary's for a pint of plain. The word about Behan is that he now consists of 95% alcohol. He went to the doctor who told him that if he didn't quit his beloved 'gargle' immediately, he'd be dead within five minutes. He ignored this advice and continues to down vast quantities. Similar news on O'Nolain who now consumes 35% of Guinness' brewery output."

*Patrick Kavanagh*
*October 6th 1959*

*John Mackay's Law Of Budgetary Omnipotence:*

*(No. 9 in a series)*

*Every crowd has a silver lining*

## Mackay decides to oppose divorce referendum

## Red Rose Estate say no to saying no to divorce

### October 7: On This Day

Do ya think I'm sexy?

I got home today, and had a chat with the family
about my new philosophy of life. They all agree that I have put up
with too much from the Red Rose Estate lot. Dreamer Lingus,
divorce referendums, bunburger tribunals, judicial job-juggling, having to
remember to say strategic alliance when I mean privatisation...
well, I'M MAD AS HELL AND I'M NOT GOING TO TAKE IT ANY MORE.
I called round to Dickie today and told him Tom Dickorharry was
getting the Neighbourhood Watch job and I was no longer going to
support the divorce referendum. He was a bit shocked, and
convened an emergency Red Rose Estate Workshop where they
all recited Prayer For Divorce
Number Four:

### RED ROSE ESTATE PRAYER FOR DIVORCE NUMBER FOUR

Divorce is so good for young children
They can sharpen the end of a comb
And stab their teacher in the leg
And blame their broken home

8/9

but I remained adamant
that, despite this obvious advantage, I had changed my mind on the
issue and I was not the sort of person to change my mind again.
For I am now a Global Statesman With A Tan. And life is good.

> **When a person says that he agrees with something in principle, it means that he hasn't got the slightest intention of doing it in practice**

*- Otto Von Bismark*

John Mackay's "Things Not To Say" - (No. 37 in a series)

Things Not To Say To Gerry Ryan:

"Bon joorie Monsewer Gary, dooz ponts poor votra Fronsezz"

6 billion

**October 10: On This Day**

Feast of funny things

Half moon visible at night time only

Hot water invented, 1932

**New policy plan for Emerald Meadows**

**Olé days are back as Euro-soccer campaign returns**

**October 12: On This Day**

First inaccurate weather forecast broadcast on tv, 1950

**Monday 10**

Had a word today with Bertie Bucks, an tAthair Smith, Maire Go Go and Riffo Cowen about the philosophical questions that have been whirling round in my head since the Runway to Damascus incident. While they were all a bit hazy on the wider issues of life, the afterlife, Plato, and Aristotle, Bertie said he'll have a go at figuring out why the BBC can't accept that the referee was wrong to allow Geoff Hurst's second goal in the 1966 World Cup final. And none of them could figure out why we've put up with all

**Tuesday 11**

that crap, total crap, from the Red Rose Estate lot for so long. So we decided to go back to our roots – Emerald Meadows, Ourselves Alone – and we've given ourselves two weeks to come up with a new policy document, provisionally titled "There Is A Better Way – The Way Backwards". Meanwhile, tomorrow we play our second European Championship match, against the footballing might of Liechtenstein.

## THE PADDY COX HA HA HA GUIDE TO GREAT FOOTBALL CHANTS OF OUR TIME

Where's your father, where's your father, where's your father, referee, you haven't got one, you never had one, you're a policeman, refereee

> **My philosophy is simple. If you see a snake, you kill it. You don't form a committee to talk about it**
>
> *- Ross Perot*

<u>John Mackay's</u>
<u>"Things Not To Say"</u> -

(No. 38 in a series)

Things Not To Say To
Des O'malley As he
Rushes To Catch What
he Has Been Told Is
The 8.05 Train To Belfast For An
All Party Oireachtas Meeting
With Unionist Councillors :

"The 7.55 to Belfast is now
leaving from Platform 4 "

6 billion

---

**October 13: On This Day**

Faulty sand withdrawn from Achill beach, 1966

Censorship banned in Cuba, 1960

**Red Rose Estate take firm line on divorce poll**

**October 15: Diary Entry**

"I went out to the garden to pick daisies this morning. The garden is very pretty. I saw a ladybird when I was in the garden. It was very pretty too. In the afternoon, I thought I might go and feed the birds in the park, but I changed my mind at the last moment and went out and shot a couple of protestants instead."

*Dominic McGlinchy*
*October 15, 1980*

Yesterday was a close match against Liechtenstein – **Thursday 13**
too close. We scraped through 4-0 with two goals from
a former international recalled to the squad after a spell in
television commentary. In fact, as Toby pointed out, it was
Dunphy's first ever goals for Ireland. Dickie Mandate called round
today to give me a copy of a motion passed by the Red Rose
Estate lot at another of their emergency mid-term policy
think-in meetings in Killiney:

## MOTION PASSED AT RED ROSE ESTATE THINK-IN

The Red Rose Estate Comrades, noting
and condemning the pro-establishment
collaboration of the Capitalist Running
Dog Lackeys of the Emerald Meadows
Bourgeoisie, hereby resolve that we will
stay in partnership with them anyway
since, basically, we're fucked if we don't.

I had another word with **Sat ... 15/16**
Dickie's lot today. They've agreed to give Tom Dickorharry the
judicial job, to forget about the divorce referendum, to privatise
the public phone in the community centre, and to agree with my
version ... of the .... bunburger ... tribunal. However, when I suggested
privatising the secretarial services for the C.R.A.P. meetings, Dickie
freaked completely and started shouting something about his
fundamental duty to protect the inalienable rights of the family.

**I don't like strident women**

*- Margaret Thatcher*

John Mackay's Anthology Of Really Crap Jokes I Heard In The Pub This Year:

(No. 13 in a series)

Those infamous photos of Fergie, before she married Andrew, were originally mislaid at the chemist where she had sent them to be developed. But Fergie refused to believe they were lost, always insisting that one day her prints would come.

6 billion

**October 17: On This Day**

Campaign to keep Limerick two hundred miles from Dublin begins, 1967

Religious fervour whipped up for first time after child pushes monk down hole, 1325

**October 18: On This Day**

Chain smoking linked to cigarettes for first time, 1960

Plans to rebuild Ennis with lego proposed, 1890

**Drama as Dickie Mandate walks out of coalition**

Well, I don't believe it. It finally happened. Judgement Day.
The Red Rose Estate lot have walked out of the C.R.A.P. Committee.
Dickie explained that, purely as a matter of principle, they couldn't
jeopardize the jobs of their family members, as it might be
misinterpreted as symbolising that they didn't care about the jobs
of other families. And he said it with a perfectly
straight face.

Today was an intensely emotional day,
so I channelled my energies into writing the following psalm

ODE ON THE TRAUMATIC OCCASION OF
DICKIE MANDATE WALKING OUT ON US

© John Mackay 1994

The temporary little
Arrangement has passed
THANK GOD ALMIGHTY
WE'RE FREE AT LAST !!!!!!

Today is the second day of our freedom from the Red Rose Estate
lot. And, fortunately, it's only mid October, which means the C.R.A.P.
Committee is still on its summer holidays. So we've still got some
time yet before we have to start worrying about how we'll cope
without them. I think we'll do okay.

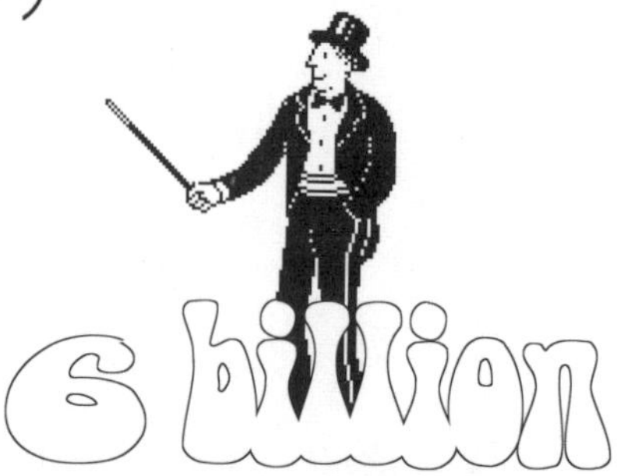

**October 20: On This Day**

Cynthia Ní Murchú and Clare McKeon instigate major inquiry after guest gets word in edgeways on Suite Talk, 1994

Maureen Potter performs miracle at supermarket, 1976

Fire discovered, 345 b.c.

" Gaeity is
the most
outstanding feature
of the Soviet
Union "

*- Joseph Stalin*

John Mackay's
"Things Not To Say" -
(No. 39 in a series)

Things Not To Say
To Martin Cullen:

Before you start
on that typing and
filing, could you
make Mary a cup
of tea, love? Milk, two sugars.
By the way, you look gorgeous
today "

## Speculation on return of political stalwarts

## Mackay continues to develop new philosophy of life

**October 22: On This Day**

They just don't want to work

6 billion

# CRAP

## the Combined Residents Association Partnership

### between Emerald Meadows and the Red Rose Corporation Estate

Minutes of C.R.A.P. meeting, October 1994

1. The Chairman, Mr John Mackay, expressed his ~~relief~~ regret that the Red Rose Corporation Estate had left the Partnership. Everyone present ~~cheered~~ agreed.

2. The Committee examined the first draft of the Emerald Meadows policy document, "There Is A Better Way – The Way backwards". Its main proposal so far is trying to make condoms illegal again. An tAthair Smith suggested as a slogan "Cops Should Chase Rubbers Not Robbers", and wondered whether Queen Mary might be asked to launch the campaign. The chairman said he would ask Brian to give her a ring.

3. The Chairman, Mr Mackay, asked the Committee for suggestions on how to replace the Red Rose Estate members of the Committee. It was agreed that some of the older residents, who used to be on the Committee in the past, should be approached. The chairman undertook to speak to Mr Sean Buacaire and Papa Rambo Burke.

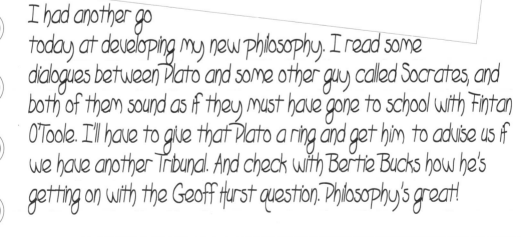

I had another go today at developing my new philosophy. I read some dialogues between Plato and some other guy called Socrates, and both of them sound as if they must have gone to school with Fintan O'Toole. I'll have to give that Plato a ring and get him to advise us if we have another Tribunal. And check with Bertie Bucks how he's getting on with the Geoff Hurst question. Philosophy's great!

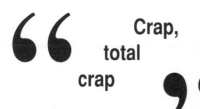

**Crap,
total
crap**

*- Albert Reynolds*

John Mackay's
"Things Not To Say" -

(No. 40 in a series)

Things Not To Say To John
Alderdice When he Complains
About Albert Ignoring
The Alliance Party:

" Here's the plan,
John. Send Philip
McGarry out to
shoot someone, then
issue a statement
renouncing violence "

**October 24: Diary Entry**

"What does the 'D' in my name stand for? I am determined to find out. Will look into the feasibility of setting up a special sub-committee (all Irish speaking, of course) to investigate the issue. I shall hope that it stands for something in Irish, like 'Daithí' or even 'Dearbhla', but I shall not be overly upset if it stands for 'Donal'. Perhaps I can employ some young Irish film maker to record the proceedings and then show it on my all Irish language television station?"

*Michael D Higgins*
*October 24 1994*

# Mackay begins new recruitment drive

# Breakthrough in new Mackay philosophy of life

*I called down today to Sean Buacaire's house to ask him to come back onto the C.R.A.P. Committee. Sean wasn't there, but I talked to his brother, who was building a small but very attractive security wall around the house. He said he'd ask Sean to ring me when he got back – he's a great man for using the telephone, is Sean.*

# CRAP

## the Combined Residents Association Partnership

### between Emerald Meadows and the Red Rose Corporation Estate

Minutes of Emergency C.R.A.P. meeting, October 1994

1. The emergency meeting was convened when Mr Bertie Bucks told the Chairman, Mr Mackay, that he had come up with the answer to the Geoff Hurst second goal question. After exhaustive examination of the issue, Mr Bucks has concluded that Mr Hurst's third goal should have been disallowed as well, since there were fans on the pitch at the time. Which means that the true score was two all. So England have never actually won the World Cup. Mr Riffo Cowen pointed out that, if England have never won the World Cup, then "Big" Jack never won his World Cup medal – which means he should never have become manager of Ireland. The Committee immediately realised that, in the national interest, they would have to cover this up before Eamon Dunphy found out, so Mr Bucks was asked to draft a statement on the establishment of the Geoff Hurst Second Goal Tribunal. It was the general view of those present that this should keep the lid on it for three or four years at least.

66 **Reagan won because he ran against Jimmy Carter. Had he run unopposed, he would have lost** 99

*- Mort Sahl*

Sean Buacaire rang today to say he was too busy to come back on the Committee, what with building the security wall round his house and all that. He seemed surprised when I told him he could apply for a grant to pay for the building of the wall – he's quite innocent in such matters.

**October 27: On This Day**

Custer's second last stand, 1875

Vasco de Gama hands Belmullet back to the Indians, 1478

## New Emerald Meadows policy plan ready

**October 29: On This Day**

Ireland relinquishes claim on China in return for Rockall, 1969

Trees invented, 13 b.c.

We had a look today at the final draft of our new policy plan, "The Way Backwards". We all agreed that it captures the essence of our traditional appeal as The True Neighbourhood Movement.

## EMERALD MEADOWS DRAFT POLICY PLAN - "THE WAY BACKWARDS"

1. Restoration of An Gaeilge as our official cúpla focal
2. No more coalitions*
3. Loads of athletic maidens coming at every crossroads
4. Fair tenure, fixity of freedom and whatever the other F was
5. No more coalitions*
6. Abolition of foreign games, unless with foreign managers
7. Abolition of rates and road tax and all the rest of that 1977 stuff
8. No more coalitions*
9. Loads of land rezoning
10. Whatever else we see when we look into our hearts

\* unless we need to stay in power

" **If I had been indulging in nepotism, I would have employed my wife's cousin as well** "

*- Emmet Stagg defending his giving state jobs to his daughter and his cousin*

Wednesday Nov 2:
Gumshoe McDuel got all legalistic today and insisted that we have to hold an immediate election to the C.R.A.P. Committee, so I gave my old friend Brian a ring for some advice, but the line was engaged.

**October 31: On This Day**

Last day of October, 1974

Sex without looking at a manual attempted for first time, 1678

**Blues Brothers launch policy manifesto today**

**Progressive Detectives call for early election**

**November 2: On This Day**

Feast of All Souls

Bring your own drink

The Blues Brothers have finally finished their Renewal Think-In from FA Cup Final day. Today they unveiled their own ten point plan to put Johnny in the top seat:

## BLUES BROTHERS DRAFT POLICY PLAN - "THE JUST UNIMAGINABLE"

1. Get more votes

2. Law and order *

3. A Constitutional Crusade to outlaw spending money

4. Get the trains running on time

5. More law and order *

6. Bring Back Charlie

7. Airline Timetables as a compulsory Leaving Cert subject

8. Even more law and order *

9. A Constitutional Crusade to outlaw Tallaght

10. Charisma implant and larynx by-pass

* absolutely no exceptions

/ 2

**It's a very good question, very direct, and I'm not going to answer it**

*- George Bush*

<u>John Mackay's Anthology Of Really Crap Jokes I Heard In The Pub This Year:</u>

(No. 14 in a series)

Albert Reynolds comes back to Longford with his new honorary degree in Australian economics. The local farmers ask him if he's learned anything that might be useful to them, and Albert says "buy deer, sell sheep"

**November 3: Diary Entry**

"I am begining to suspect that there are some elements in the Church which are oposed to my proposed liberal reforms. When I woke up this morning there was a bloke in my room with a big knife. I asked him what he was doing and he said that he was hunting mice and had wandered into the wrong room by mistake. I have also been shot at on several occasions. My food constantly tastes funny and yesterday I discovered several sticks of dynamite in my wardrobe. Something very strange is going on..."

*Pope John Paul I*
*November 3 1978*

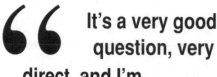

Johnny Blues calls for Rainbow Collision

**November 4: On This Day**

Backs introduced to chairs, 1665

We finally conceded today that we would have to have another election to the C.R.A.P. Committee. I asked the remainder of the Committee for ideas for our election slogan. An tAthair Smith suggested "Health Cuts Hurt The Old, The Poor And The Handicapped", but Bertie Bucks pointed out that we shouldn't have a slogan promising health cuts unless we were going to implement them. So everyone agreed that we would have to implement health cuts.

**DREAMER LINGUS**

## LATEST NEWSFLASH

Fifteen minutes after today's General Election announcement, Disruptions resumed at Dublin Airport. The Dreamer Lingus workers taxied into town in a Boeing 707 that they had commandeered from the airport, parked it sideways across the main street at rush hour then set it on fire and ran away laughing loudly and breaking car windows. "We don't want to inconvenience the public" said a union spokesperson, "But what else can we do?"

**Friday 4**

**5/6**

Johnny Blues today launched his election campaign with a plea for a Rainbow Collision of the Blues Brothers, the Red Rose Estate, the Progressive Detectives and whatever Promises de Russia's lot are calling themselves these days. He argued forcefully that the unusual combination would work, since a bird never flew on one wing, though Dympna pointed out that a bird never got far with four wings all flying in different directions.

"

**About ten minues before the announcement in the Dail, I got a call to go to the Taoiseach's office. He wanted to assure me that he had sent me a Christmas Card. He had a list of names on a typed sheet of paper with their names ticked off**

"

*- Mary Harney on Charles J. Haughey's Christmas Card list (the announcement in the Dail ten minutes later was about Dick Burke becoming European Commissioner)*

**6 billion**

**November 7: On This Day**

Hens develop feathers as protection against cold showers, 1767

Branches of trees gently blown by light breeze for first time, 1367

**November 8: On This Day**

Michael Jackson shows early signs of dancing ability, 1962

First buried treasure buried, 897

**Sean Buacaire agrees to return to Committee**

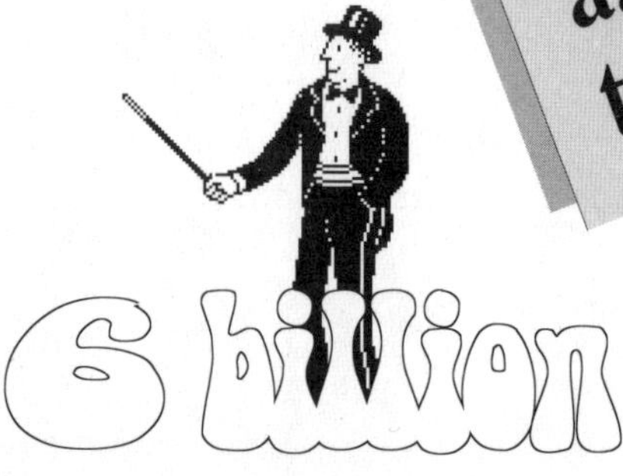

I went out for a drink tonight with Sean Buacaire, to try to persuade him to come back onto the C.R.A.P. Committee. Then, at about half twelve, the pub was raided by the local guards. It was pandemonium. Come on, Sean, I said, if you were back on the Committee we could call this a political meeting and they'd drop all the charges - or summons us from Cahirciveen. And he thought about it for a while, then agreed to come back.

**Tuesday 8**

A SHORT POEM PENNED AFTER A LONG DISCUSSION ABOUT HOW THE MEDIA ALWAYS JUDGES POLITICIANS USING SIMPLISTIC MORAL STANDARDS SUCH AS "RIGHT" AND "WRONG"

PERSECUTION IS COMPLEX

(c) John Mackay 1994

They're always saying it's my fault
They point at me and use
Their new phrase (son of GUBU
for the Euro age) - "J'ECUs"

**ay 9**

It's funny how elections affect people.
For the past few years, the residents down at Skelly Place have been promised trees outside their houses. And now, with an election coming up, it's all they're interested in. They say they won't vote for us unless they get the trees by election day. Papa Rambo Burke said he'd have a word with them, but they seem quite determined. Although so did he. We'll wait and see what happens.

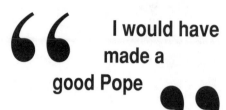

**I would have made a good Pope**

*- Richard Nixon*

John Mackay's "Things Not To Say" -

(No. 41 in a series)

Things Not To Have Said To John Giles When He And Jack Charlton Were Playing For Leeds, And Indulging In Tackles The Purpose Of Which Was Euphemistically Described As "Letting Your Opponents Know That You Were There ":

" Can you stop it there now, please ? "

6 billion

### November 10: Diary Entry

"Found a note in Dev's diary today that indicates he was considering putting a picture of himself on the Irish flag. *Very* interesting. Shall raise this intriguing snippet of information at tomorrow's cabinet meeting as a preamble to a suggestion that my own visage should appear on the tricolour. As usual, anyone who tries to stop me will be immediately fucked out of the Party. That will set me up nicely for the Ard Fheis when the topic of coinage will be discussed. I think a nice profile of old C.J. on the 50p piece will suitably impress my wine-drinking fellow heads of state in the E.C."

*Charles J. Haughey*
*November 10, 1981*

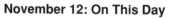

**Dreamer Lingus campaign causes major disruption**

### November 12: On This Day

Ennis destroyed in earthquake, 1867

Funerals. That's what Sean Buacaire said when I asked him the secret of getting so many votes. Being there, and making sure that no other candidates know about it. Then we bumped into Johnny Blues who told us that there was a funeral on at the local church today! We thanked him and had a good laugh at his innocence as we donned our black rosettes and set off. Unfortunately, we arrived on time, so we had to wait until everyone else had gone in so that they'd all look around and see us walking in late (as we

**Friday 11**

always say, there's no point in being in Church if nobody knows but God). After the funeral, we shook hands with the widow, and Sean asked her whether Johnny Blues had been there. Yes, the widow replied, in fact he called to the house last night. Good, said Sean, because I told him to make sure he called to you and he's been a bit unreliable lately. (this story adapted from an anecdote last retold in the John Waters classic "Praising Sean Doherty At The Crossroads.")

DREAMER LINGUS

## LATEST NEWSFLASH

In an unexpected development today, the Dreamer Lingus workers intensified their campaign. They waited for the local bin-lorry to be loaded with rubbish, then they waved it in through the glass doors of the local shopping centre using those roundy little table-tennis bats that they used to use on aircraft carriers in war films. "We don't want to inconvenience the public" said a union spokesperson, "But what else can we do?"

**"** I want to assure Orla Guerin she'll get nothing from me except the warmest co-operation and cordiality **"**

*- Bernie Malone*

John Mackay's
"Things Not To Say" -
(No. 42 in a series)
Things Not To Say To
Joe Duffy:

"I bet you used to really hate it when the Gay Byrne Show used to be attacked every day by leftist student radicals who were just out of prison ... "

6 billion

**November 14: Diary Entry**

"It all seems such a long time ago now."

*Historian A.J.P. Taylor remembers the Bronze Age, November 14, 1966*

# Windsor Park match relieves election tensions

**November 16: On This Day**

South Africa bans sugar free gum, 1970

Protestants have sex for first time, 1656

Things are looking good for the election - with one exception. Bertie Bucks told me today that the residents down at Skelly Place are definitely not going to vote for us since they still haven't got those damned trees planted outside their stupid houses. I'll have to remember to check with Papa Rambo Burke whether he has had a word with them yet.

**DREAMER LINGUS**

## LATEST NEWSFLASH

The Dreamer Lingus workers further intensified their campaign today. They selected seven volunteers from the general public, dismembered them with a blunt disembowelling cutlass, doused them in airplane fuel then symbolically set them alight after boiling their blood and drinking it at midnight under a full moon. "We don't want to inconvenience the public," said a union spokesperson, "But what else can we do?"

### Wednesday 16

Football fever again today - another European Championship match against the boys from the Norn Iron Shipyard. Now that peace has broken out, they're having trouble reconciling the views of their new power-sharing co-managers. "Big "Ian (no relation to " Big "Jack) wants to play eleven defenders, while his co-manager Mad Uncle Gerry insists that, while he recognises the right of the team to play football, he cannot in any way speak for them and has no control over their actions.

**You'd be surprised. They're all individual countries**

*- Ronald Reagan, after a trip to Latin America*

John Mackay's "Things Not To Say" -

(No. 43 in a series)

Things Not To Say To Dick Spring When He Insists On being A Revolving Taoiseach:

"Then you could have a summit with Ross Perot as Rotating President of America - your share of the national vote is exactly the same as his"

**November 17: On This Day**

Bank holiday in Burma

Eamon Dunphy martyred at Dublin Airport, 1990

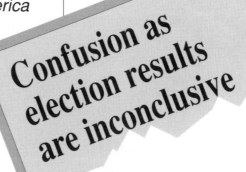

Confusion as election results are inconclusive

**November 18: On This Day**

Mars lies in Jupiter (what the fuck does that mean?)

**November 20: On This Day**

Rome surrenders to Wyatt Earp, 1878

Ice Age enters third week, 56,770,067 b.c.

**Thursday 17**

Election day! I was up all the previous night, having spent from 2 a.m. to 5 a.m. phoning residents and loudly asking them to vote for the Blues Brothers. Then at 6 a.m. I went for a stroll down Skelly Place, where the residents had been complaining about the absence of trees, and to my utter surprise, I found several workmen planting nice trees in front of the houses. Nice one, Papa Rambo Burke - though, of course, such a thing could NEVER happen in real life! The rest of the day was as busy as usual - last

**Friday 18**

minute canvassing, tearing down Dickie Mandate's posters from the railings outside the polling booth, arranging to give lifts at five minutes before closing time to elderly residents who wanted to vote for the Blues Brothers, then not turning up, that sort of thing. I can tell you, democracy is a very tiring business. So now to sleep, and we'll be back in power by the weekend.

## ELECTION NEWSFLASH

**20**

Today's C.R.A.P. election result has proved inconclusive, creating a hung Residents Association Committee. Initial reactions: Dickie Mandate has said he wants to be a rotating chairman, Mary Harmony has said she'll rotate with anyone at all except Promises de Russia, Johnny Blues is wandering around singing "Somewhere Over The Rainbow", and the Eco-Warriors are insisting that there should be no chairbeing at all. It's total chaos.

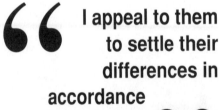

> ## I appeal to them to settle their differences in accordance with Christian principles

*- Liam Cosgrave to the Jews and the Muslims*

John Mackay's Anthology Of Really Crap Jokes I Heard In The Pub This Year:

(No. 15 in a series)

Two termites go into a pub, and one says to the other "where's the bar tender?"

### November 21: On This Day

Sex-change tennis player retires after "I'm not the player I used to be" confession, 1987

River Shannon reaches the sea for first time, 1648

## Mackay goes to Edinburgh to seek Euro funding

### November 22: Diary Entry

"I felt unwell in the morning and collapsed in the afternoon. Was rushed to hospital and felt slightly better by tea time. According to the doctors I had been suffering from a severe case of self deprecation. I missed some games at the end of last year when I went down with a touch of modesty, but this is more serious. The nurses and doctors are all very nice here, and as part of my therapy I am being encouraged to say nasty things about Wimbledon."

*Gary Liniker*
*November 22 1986*

## ELECTION NEWSFLASH

The Blues Brother leader, Mr Johnny Blues threw a bit of a wobbler today when Mr Austin Currie suggested that, if Squeaky Suds was good enough to do the cat deal and be President of the European Piggybank, then why shouldn't he take over from Johnny as Chairman of the Blues Brothers? After some debate, everyone accepted that getting reins on the Blues Brothers was a far more difficult job than putting a ceiling on the CAP.

22

The residents from Skelly Place were up in arms today, complaining about the trees that were planted outside their houses on the morning of the election. It seems they've been dug up and taken back again - but then we wouldn't know anything about that. Thankfully, I had to go to Edinburgh for a meeting of the European Piggybank to decide on our grants for the next few years.

**Wednesday 23**

The European Piggybank meeting went great - we've been offered over six billion pounds! Then we had a wonderful meal with food from every European country. I was halfway through some Greek squid when Bertie Bucks told me it was an octopus and I was halfway through one of its testicles. Then I threw up all over some American guy called Bush, but he was very understanding, and said it could happen to anyone.

**" It was five per cent patriotism and ninety five per cent ego "**

*- Robert Strauss on why he accepted the post of US Ambassador to Moscow*

John Mackay's
"Things Not To Say" -

(No. 44 in a series)

Things Not To Say
When You're A
Boxing Referee And
The Progressive
Democrats
Parliamentary Party
Is In The Audience:

" Ten, nine, eight, seven, six ... "

**November 24: On This Day**

Vision of Mike Murphy appears on gable wall of Knock church, 1899

Women shave underarm hair for first time, 1678

## Mackay gets guarantee of £6b in Euro-funds

## £8 billion bonanza "in the bag" says jubilant Mackay

**November 24: On This Day**

Suspension of belief lifted after year long protest, 1945

A SHORT POEM INSPIRED BY THE AMAZINGLY LARGE AND
ENORMOUS AMOUNT OF MONEY THAT WE'VE BEEN GIVEN BY
THE EUROPEAN PIGGYBANK, WHICH IS SUCH A BRILLIANT
DEVELOPMENT THAT EVEN I COULDN'T MESS IT UP !!!!!!

ODE TO THE SIX BILLION POUNDS

© John Mackay 1994

Six billion pounds - and scandal-proof!
And we don't even have to spoof!
Six billion pounds - it's really great!
It couldn't be better if it were eight!

**25**

I got back from
Edinburgh today, and Dickie Mandate
and Ruari Rua asked me how I got on. So I said, well I ate brilliant
squid, and Dickie said "Eight billion quid? that's brilliant news!". And Ruari
Rua said "I thought you got six?" And I remembered my dramatic
technicolour yawn during the dinner and said, well, yeah, for a while
but not now. Then they both rushed off laughing to have another of
their Emergency Red Rose Estate Policy Workshops.

**Sat/Sun 26/27**

I don't know how, but it's all round the neighbourhood
today that I got eight billion pounds, not six billion, in Edinburgh. I
asked Bertie Bucks what we should do and he said, "Well, nobody I
know can count that high anyway, so just go along with it".
Dympna said she has a feeling it might cause some complications
later on, but, sure, if things get out of hand we can always establish
a tribunal or something. So let's go for it!

> **Those who have committed themselves by joining the PDs have done so very fully**

*- Michael Keating*

John Mackay's "Things Not To Say" - (No. 45 in a series)

Things Not To Say To The Birmingham Six Or The Guildford Four:

" Ah, but be fair now, they <u>did</u> let you out once they realised they had made a mistake "

**November 28: Diary Entry**

Last week of November nears end

Two legged trousers introduced, 1690

## Mackay agrees new terms with Dickie Mandate

**November 30: Diary Entry**

"A light mist descended on me in the morning. By mid afternoon it was a dense fog. When I arrived in for afternoon tea I was soaked through to the skin. Lady Gregory took one look at me and immediately decided that my appearance had given her inspiration for a play. She disappeared into her study immediately and did not emerge until ten, at which point she declared herself immensely happy with the first act. By this time Synge had arrived, completely covered in dung and full of enthusiasm about a peasant he had been assaulted by in Clifden the previous day."

*W.B. Yeats at Coolepark*
*November 30 1909*

**Monday 28**

Well, it's nearly December, so our Summer holidays are drawing to a close. Next week we have our first meeting of the new C.R.A.P. Committee, and Dickie and I have done a deal to continue as before. All we have to do to make up the numbers is come to some sort of arrangement with the Eco-Warriors and with young Gregory Deal, who hold the balance of power between them. I met today with the Gregorian Rant in a ramshackle old house down by Summer Hill. He says he'll vote for us if we act in the Neighbourhood Interest. And, as we know from the

**Tuesday 29**

Bunburger Tribunal, the Neighbourhood Interest is whatever you decide it is. Gregory Deal reckons it's somewhat like the following (and I tend to agree with him):

**AGREEMENT IN THE NEIGHBOURHOOD INTEREST BETWEEN MR JOHN MACKAY AND MR GREGORY DEAL**

1. Fifty per cent of the C.R.A.P. budget goes to making improvements in Mr Gregory Deal's street.

2. The other fifty per cent of the C.R.A.P. budget goes to making improvements in Mr Gregory Deal's street.

**30**

3. If there's anything left over after that, it goes to making improvements in Mr Gregory Deal's street.

4. Mr Gregory Deal votes for Mr John Mackay as Chairman.

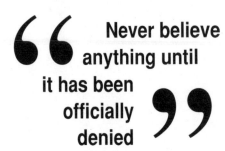

" Never believe
anything until
it has been
officially
denied "

*- Otto Von Bismarck*

John Mackay's
"Things Not To Say" -
(No. 46 in a series)

Things Not To Say To
Patricia McKenna:

"If you were serious
about your ecological
credentials, you'd
swim over to Brussels
instead of taking an
airplane "

### December 1: On This Day

Woman falls thirty thousand feet into
Cavan pothole, 1967

Neandarthal man breaks into trot for
first time, 878,000 b.c.

## Mackay and Johnny Blues woo Eco-Warriors

### December 2: On This Day

Battle of Waterloo "still some years
away" declares Napoleon, 1807

### December 3: On This Day

Left footed people banned from
Coloseum, 78 b.c.

I met the Eco-warriors today. They say the Committee shouldn't have a chairbeing at all! Instead they want everyone to sit on a large soyabeanbag which would mould itself into the shape of our collective spiritual aura, with everyone taking and sharing inner responsibility for chairing their own contribution to the consensual dialogue. I said I'd get back to them later, as frankly I haven't a clue what they're on about.

## NEWSFLASH - NO ENTRY TODAY

Mr John Mackay today failed to make an entry in his diary amidst rumours that he couldn't think of anything to write. His wife Dympna is believed to have suggested that he write an entry about not being able to think of anything to write, but Mr Mackay is understood to have pointed out that he had already done this once back in August, and he would never get away with it twice. (unless, perhaps, if he did the second one as a newsflash instead of a diary entry)

3/4

I hear that Johnny Blues had a meeting today with the Eco-Warriors. They explained to Johnny their philosophical preference for a consensual and non-adversarial method of conducting the affairs of the Committeee, and Johnny explained that HE WAS GOING TO BE CHAIRMAN BECAUSE HE HAD THE MOST SEATS AND HIS DADDY WAS BIGGER THAN THEIRS AND THEY COULD GET STUFFED IF THEY DIDN'T LIKE IT !!!!

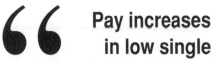
**Pay increases in low single figures will have to be accepted**

*- Finance Minister Alan Dukes before a 19% pay increase for TDs*

*John Mackay's Universal Law Of Political Damage Limitation (Applicable To All Parties And All Situations)*

*(No. 10 in a series)*

*(a) Don't fix the problem, fix the blame*

*(b) Criticise people, not behaviour*

**December 5: On This Day**

Pandas decide on black and white colouring as ideal camoflage, 1678

Universities allow in students for first time, 1567

## Squeaky Suds in poll challenge to Johnny Blues

## Shock as Rainbow Collision takes office

**December 5: On This Day**

Day of the Triffids

## NOT REALLY NEWSFLASH: BLUES BROTHERS IN NEW LEADERSHIP CHALLENGE

There was more pressure today on Mr Johnny Blues to let Mr Sqeaky Suds be the Blues Brothers candidate for Chairman of C.R.A.P., but Mr Blues explained that it was unthinkable for any serious political grouping to consider nominating anyone other than their leader as Chairman. It had never happened before, he said. Well, not since General Eoin O'Duffy, anyway.

**y 6**

Today we had our
first meeting of the new C.R.A.P. Committee –
and what a disaster it turned out to be ! Astonishingly, the Blues
Brothers have done a deal with the Eco-Warriors to take over the
running of the Residents Association. The Chairmanship will rotate
every week between Mr Sqeaky Suds – who has resigned from his
new job as editor of the Irish Times – and an Eco-
Collective consisting of Patricia McKelangelo, John     **Wednesday 7**
Reasonable Gormley, Trevor Private, and a large
greenhouse full of ripe tomatoes. Their agreed priorities are law
and order without spending any money while protecting our
neutrality with a very large hedge along the coastline. And they're
being supported by Mary Harmony and Promises de Russia, who
have both demanded at least one day each as Chairman every
forty six years, as long as they're on the Committee.

" **I'm Peter Lilley, Secretary of State for Trade and Industry** "

*- Top Tory Peter Lilley, introducing himself at a televised Westminster Committee meeting, before being reminded that he was, in fact, Secretary of State for Social Security*

John Mackay's "Things Not To Say" -

(No. 47 in a series)

Things Not To Say To Alan Clark:

"Have you met my wife and daughters?"

**December 8: On This Day**

Amerigo Vespucci sets sail for Brazil, 1501

Amerigo Vespucci returns to port after forgetting his sandwiches, 1501 - later the same day

**December 9: On This Day**

Kildare cheese shortage enters fifth week, 1980

1066 and all that, 1066

Rainbow Collision announce agreed Plan of Action

## AGREED PROGRAMME OF ACTIVITIES FOR THE BLUES BROTHERS, ECO-WARRIORS AND OTHERS RAINBOW COLLISION

1   While the Blues Brothers are chairing the Rainbow Collision, the priority will be law and order without spending any money. Johnny Blues will be part-time Treasurer during his time off from his new job in the children's shoeshop, and Slaphead the DJ will chair the Neighbourhood Watch, with special responsibility for ensuring that anyone who disagrees with the Committee ends up in prison.

2   While the Eco-Collective is chairing the Rainbow Collision, the Committee will be disbanded and there will be a referendum every day to see what people want to do (apart from people who eat meat, or who wear clothes, or who put double glazing windows into Georgian houses, or who generally disagree with us, all of whom will be subject to Clause 1 above).

3   Mary Harmony is Honorary Chairman of the Subcommittee For Ensuring That None Of Promises de Russia's Proposals Get Implemented.

4   Promises de Russia is Honorary Chairman of the Subcommittee For Ensuring That None Of Mary Harmony's Proposals Get Implemented.

**December 12: Diary Entry**

"I tried not to be eccentric today, but it was hopeless. I felt a twinge of eccentricity around noon, and then I became increasingly eccentric during the afternoon. Around four o'clock I made a witty remark about the similarities between capitalism and zoo animals, but there was nobody in the room to hear it. I think I shall write another pamphlet tomorrow if I can think of an interesting subject. Modern traffic perhaps, or the undesirability of central heating."

*George Bernard Shaw*
*December 12, 1938*

" **Our people have not experienced incidents of this nature since the time of Cromwell** "

*- Liam Hyland on crime*

*John Mackay's Anthology Of Jokes That Are So Brilliantly Crap That They Just Had To be Included Even Though They Wouldn't Fit On One Page*

*(No. 2 in a very short series)*

**Rainbow Collision begin hard task of governing**

*A man dies and goes to Hell, the gates of which he approaches with understandable trepidation. But when he gets there, he just finds people enjoying themselves, eating, drinking and carousing. "Heaven is boring" explains Old Nick, "but in Hell, everything is exactly whatever you want it to be!"....*

*( continued on next left hand page ...)*

2 billion

**Monday 12**

And so we begin our first full week of rule by the Rainbow Collision. They seem to be dovetailing their ideologies very well. The Blues Brothers have doubled the prison population, but instead of sewing mailbags, the prisoners are being given organic gardening lessons by the Eco-Warriors, and are then being given parole to help build the very big hedge along the coast that's going to protect our neutrality (a policy which they managed to get past Squeaky Suds because he thought The Hedge was something to do with U 2 gunboats). Meanwhile, I'm having my own

**Tuesday 13**

problems. First we lose the election, now my own lot are trying to get rid of me. But fortunately, ~~Gerry~~ Gerard Collins dramatically burst into tears and pleaded with the rebels not to burst up the centre of the neighbourhood right down the middle from left to right and inside out and back to front. Naturally, they immediately recognised that they were displaying frightful political immaturity and they backed off.

## NEUTRALITY BREACHED SHOCK NEWSFLASH

There was a minor diplomatic incident at the coast today, when a small salmon leaped out of the water and over the hedge that's supposed to protect our neutrality. A tribunal was quickly convened to find out why the hedge hadn't been built tall enough, and it discovered that the Defence Forces had been using "The Big Book Of Garden Security", written by a friend of Sean Buacaire's brother.

" **We do try to anticipate your questions so that I can respond 'no comment' with some degree of knowledge** "

*- CIA spokesperson
William Baker*

**December 15: On This Day**

Love stories begin at Zhivago's, 1973

First all-chimpanzee Irish-speaking school opened in Spiddal, 1954

*(... continued from previous left hand page)*

.... The man is amazed but, sure enough, everything is just as he wants it to be - bountiful

**Mackay launches new book of political poetry**

supplies of his favourite food and drink, and every woman who he is attracted to is attracted to him also. Only one thing bothers him - the screams and wails coming from the top of a nearby mountain. Despite Satan suggesting otherwise, he decides to climb the mountain. As he nears the summit, the screams get louder and the temperature gets hotter ...

*(continued on next left hand page ...)*

2 billion

I had a great idea today. Since I've now got **Thursday 15**
more time for intellectual pursuits, I photocopied all
of my poems and stapled them together and started selling them
as "The John Mackay Book Of C.R.A.P.
Poetry"

A SHORT POEM ENCAPSULATING THE
JOHN MACKAY PHILOSOPHY ON THE
WORLD'S NUMBER ONE SPECTATOR SPORT

**CRAP**

ODE TO POLITICAL INSOMNIACS

© John Mackay 1994

**16**

If you have trouble trying to sleep
Here's something you could try
Politicians do it standing up
Because they never lie

The Blues Brothers today banned
my Book Of C.R.A.P. poetry. In fact, they've banned all literature,
under Section 31 of the Abolition Of Leisure Act, since every hour
spent reading books could otherwise be spent doing
something useful like helping to rectify the balance **Sat/Sun 17/18**
of payments deficit. And when I asked the Eco-
Collective to reverse the decision, they said that they were also
banning Christmas! They plan to replace it with an optional
celebration of identification with one's personal concept of the
relationship between deity and nature. And Santa Claus has also
been banned as an oppressive gender-stereotype of patriarchal
control of the means of production of seasonal gratification.

" **Maybe they
will find that
Flynn is a man
of vision** "

*- Padraig Flynn
on himself*

(*... continued from previous left hand page*)

... When he reaches
the top, he realises
he is looking into a
live volcano, inside
which countless
people are burning
alive as, in the heat,
their eyeballs melt and
dribble down their cheeks. The man rushes back down the
mountain and asks the Devil what the hell is going on. "I know, I
know," says Old Nick, "I don't like it any more than you do. But
it's the Catholics - they insist on it."

**December 19: Diary Entry**

"Only a couple of shopping days to
go to Christmas and I still haven't
bought anyone anything. I've just been
so busy travelling around the world
and being popular. My brilliant plan to
buy everybody in Ireland a present
was deemed to be too expensive, so I
might just knit some of them
cardigans. Oh, I do so wish that all the
Irish emigrants who live abroad could
come home at Christmas and dance
with me in the Ierne ballroom. It would
be such fun. And then maybe we
could all go to Bewleys for tea
afterwards."

*President Mary Robinson
December 19, 1993*

## Michael Wee calls
## for Poets' Rising
## against Collision

I went down to the local Poetry Workshop today,
where Michael Wee from the Red Rose Estate was reading his
latest verse: <u>Ode To The Glorious Men Of 1916</u>

```
A SHORT POEM BY MICHAEL WEE


   ODE TO THE GLORIOUS MEN OF 1916
  © Michael Wee 1994

   Oh wise men riddle me this
   What if the dream came true
   What if roses were red
   And what if violets were blue
   And what if the national debt
   Was paid off by my mates in U2 ...
```

We all told him
the second two lines might work in a
Valentines Card, but the first two lines were going nowhere. But he
said, no, wait a minute, don't you understand, beware the risen
people whose loss is somebody else's opportunity for a blood
sacrifice, or some such nonsense. Frankly, we all thought that Dessie
Candoit was right and that Michael Wee had finally gone mad, but by
the end of the evening he had talked us into holding a Poet's Rising on
Christmas Day to protest about the banning of literature. When we
pointed out the obvious flaw – that we hadn't a snowball's chance in
Orlando of winning – he said, exactly, and look at the reception Big
Jack's team got when they lost. So we said, fair enough, we're in.

" If a frog had wings, then he wouldn't hit his tail on the ground. If. Too hypothetical. "

*- George Bush, refusing to answer a hypothetical question*

John Mackay's
"Things Not To Say" -

(No. 48 in a series)

Things Not To Say To Bertie Ahern:

"It's not the size of the debt, it's that you don't know how to budge it "

**December 22: On This Day**

Chris de Burgh urges his followers to kill themselves in mass suicide pact, 1997

People look forward to Christmas, 1789

Rimbaud Cowen joins Poets for Christmas Rising

Christmas Rising cancelled until tomorrow morning

**December 25: On This Day**

Yes, it's the big one

I had a word with the lads down the pub about Michael Wee's idea for a Christmas Rising. Riffo Cowen was all on for it, but I told him he had to be a poet to join in. So he grabbed a biro and a beermat and came up with the following epic:

```
A SHORT POEM BY RIFFO COWEN
(HENCEFORTH TO BE KNOWN AS RIMBAUD COWEN)

     ODE TO THE GLORIOUS MEN OF 1916

   © Rimbaud Cowen 1994

   There's gonna be a nasty accident
   (clap, clap-clap-clap,
   clap-clap, clap, clap-clap-clap)
   You're going home by fuckin' ambulance
   (clap, clap-clap-clap,
   clap-clap, clap, clap-clap-clap)
```

I brought Rimbaud Cowen's poem round to Michael Wee today and he said, well, it's more of a football chant, really, isn't it, and I said, well, I suppose it is, but he'd be pretty handy in a revolution, and Michael Wee said okay then, he's in.

Christmas Day! We were all set for the Rising when word came through that Michael Wee wanted it cancelled because he had got a Paul Durcan book for Christmas and he wanted to read it before he died. Rimbaud Cowen was a bit upset, but we felt, fair enough, I suppose we can do it tomorrow instead. I mean, the timing isn't crucial. It's only a revolution, after all.

" I am very worry
about this,
because this
is a liar "

*- Jacques Delors*

John Mackay's
"Things Not To Say" -

(No. 49 in a series)

Things Not To Say
To The Reverend
Ian Paisley About
John Hume and
Albert Reynolds:

"Don't let that
paranoia "

**December 26: On This Day**

Night of the long knives

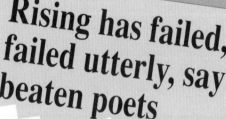

History is made as
Post Office is
stormed by poets

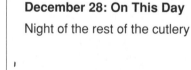

Rising has failed,
failed utterly, say
beaten poets

**December 28: On This Day**

Night of the rest of the cutlery

6 billion

**Monday 26**

Today we started the Christmas Monday Rising.
We went down to the GPO, where Rimbaud Cowen and I caused a distraction by complaining about the price of the television licences. Then Michael Wee took out his book of poetry and started reading it and everybody ran for cover. Within minutes, we were in control. The Rising had started. We were making history. We soon consolidated our position, with Sean Buacaire taking control of the public telephones while Michael Wee and I co-wrote a rousing rebel song to keep up everyone's spirits

**Tuesday 27**

```
A ROUSING REBEL SONG

       VICTORY TO THE CHRISTMAS MONDAY RISING!
    © John Mackay & Michael Wee 1994
    Soldiers are we, whose lives are pledged to
    At Boolavogue, as the sun was setting

        Olé, olé olé olé, olé olé
        Olé, olé olé olé, olé olé
        Olé, olé olé olé, olé olé
        Olé, olé olé olé, olé olé
```

**28**

The Rising ended today.
We've been holding out well enough in the Post Office and down in the Biscuit Factory, but frankly the public seemed on the verge of losing sympathy with the Dreamer Lingus Battallion, who had brought in British gunboats to bomb the Airport Road. Michael Wee wrote our formal surrender terms: "We don't want to inconvenience the public " he wrote, "so we're not going to. "

**December 29: Diary Entry**

"Plans for my all Irish language television station are going very well. I met a man in Clare yesterday who said he might look at it. So that's me, him, and two old age pensioners in Spiddal. Not a bad start. We could be in double figures by the end of the century."

*Michael D Higgins*
*December 29, 1994*

" We just don't discuss that capability ... I can't tell you why, because then I'd be discussing it "

*- American Defence Spokesperson on missile use in the Gulf War*

John Mackay's "Things Not To Say" -

(No. 50 in a series)

Things Not To Say At A Former H - Block Dirty Protest Prisoners Reunion:

"I see it's just the same old familiar faeces again"

## Glorious defeat is transformed into dramatic victory

## Mackay confronts spirits of elections past & future

**December 31: On This Day**
Last day of 1969, 1969

I'm writing today's entry from the darkest depths of a very deep and dark dungeon indeed. The Rising has failed, failed utterly. – all around is devastation, with only the Dreamer Lingus Battalion still fighting on. And, to make things worse, the perfidious Blues Brothers have publicly burned all copies of My Book Of C.R.A.P. Poetry, – together with the British telephone directory, which they discovered has telephone numbers of foreign bookshops.

All has changed, changed utterly. As is the tradition with the Boys In Green – at Dublin 1916 and Italia 1990 – we are now seen by the begrudgers to have succeeded in our cunningly disguised aim of being gloriously defeated. We had a brief celebratory parade in the prison yard, ending with a standing ovation for our newly elected Chairman and Patron Of All Things Creative And Artistic, The Spirit Of The Neighbourhood and Our Future Emperor, The Great Lord Charles J Haughty. A terrible Cutie is born.

I have just discovered that it is not the end of December, but the end of September, and that I am still standing on the runway at Shannon, waiting for Boris The Red to appear. It seems that, when I was blinded by the sun glistening on that vodka bottle, I went into a deep trance and have been visited by the Spirits of Elections Past and Elections Future. I should have realised – the events since then have lacked the credibility and reality of the year's first nine months ....

# Notes

## Dear Me - The Index

Note: Entries are listed by the date on the top right hand corner of the double page spread on which they appear

Index: Entries are listed by the date on the top right hand corner of the double page spread on which they appear

# Notes

# Notes

# Notes

# Notes